Murder in New Orleans

A Mallory Beck Cozy Culinary Caper (Book 8)

Denise Jaden

Denise Jaden Books

MURDER IN NEW ORLEANS

First Edition. December, 2021.

Cover Design: Novak Illustration

Cover Illustrations: Ethan Heyde

Written by Denise Jaden

Murder in New Orleans

A Mallory Beck culinary travel mystery

A food tour in New Orleans where murder is on the menu...

When Mallory Beck wins a food tour experience in New Orleans, she invites teenage Amber, her foodie BFF, to join her on a road trip of French and creole cuisine. Mallory's cat-sitter cancels at the last minute, and presumptuous, cheeky Hunch helps himself to shotgun in

Mallory's Prius. A good thing, too, because when a know-it-all food tour participant turns up dead and wrapped in Mardi Gras beads, they'll need Hunch's keen nose to sniff out any foul play.

Surrounded by tight-lipped locals and voodoo theories, Mallory and her team of sleuths have their work cut out for them to clear Amber's name from suspicion and get to the bottom of what happened to the Po' Boy who didn't make it through to the last stop on the food tour.

Join my mystery readers' newsletter today!

Sign up now, and you'll get access to a special mystery to accompany this series—an exclusive bonus for newsletter subscribers. In addition, you'll be the first to hear about new releases and sales, and receive special excerpts and behind-the-scenes bonuses.
Visit the link below to sign up and receive your bonus mystery:

https://www.subscribepage.com/
mysterysignup

Chapter One

IT WAS SIX O'CLOCK in the morning and I was already talking a blue streak to my ornery cat.

"Listen, Hunch, you'll like Seth. I promise. He's related to Amber, so how bad could he be, right?" Using my sixteen-year-old BFF's name made Hunch pause from his pacing along the backseat of my white Prius. In truth, I didn't know much about Amber's older brother, Seth. "You'll have to stay in his room because their mom is allergic to all things fur-covered, but Seth goes out all the time. He'll take you with him."

This was a guess, but apparently, Seth liked animals. I'd at least asked that much.

When I pulled into the driveway of Amber's mom's mansion, the sun's glow was barely peeking over the horizon. The town felt dark and quiet so I turned off my engine and picked up my phone to text Amber.

Should I bring Hunch in or does Seth want to come out and get him?

Three dots appeared. I waited a long time for two words to appear.

About that...

I stared at my phone, but no more dots appeared. Even Hunch sensed something was wrong and climbed onto the console to nuzzle up to my shoulder —a good deal more affection than my late husband's cat usually gave me. I didn't believe animals could read, and yet, I clearly wasn't convinced because I flashed him my phone screen so he could have a peek.

He let out a mix between a mewl and a growl.

"I know." I stroked his head, accepting the rare opportunity when he'd let me give him some love. Still, the dots indicating her reply didn't appear. "I have a bad feeling about this, too—"

A knock on the passenger window made me slap a hand to my chest as my heart skipped a beat and then pounded. But it was only Amber. I'd neglected to unlock her door.

She opened the door, but didn't get in. A red and white duffel bag sat at her feet, and she wore a black hoodie that read: THAT'S A HORRIBLE IDEA. WHAT TIME?

I didn't notice her frown until she picked up Hunch and cuddled him to her neck. He immediately started purring.

"Bad news, Hunchie." Amber was the only one who could get away with cutesy nicknames with my cat.

"What? What bad news?" I strained my neck to see the dark upper rooms of the Montrose mansion. "Where's Seth?"

My hope deflated before I even had the question out. I'd been looking forward to this road trip for months. After Amber had entered a cooking contest at school, she'd caught the bug for competition and insisted I enter Foodie Elite Magazine's original recipe contest. The food tour I'd won tickets to in New Orleans had high ratings in all the food magazines, and I'd heard great things even before I won the tickets.

"Seth can't take Hunch?" I guessed because Amber still hadn't answered me.

"Seth can't take Hunch," she echoed into my cat's fur.

Hunch wasn't the type of cat you could drop off at any old pet kennel. Hunch had been my mystery-author-husband's assistant before he passed, and I often suspected the cat had a bigger brain than I did. He wouldn't last a day in a cage without a single stimulating human conversation.

And it would dishonor Cooper's memory to put Hunch in such a place.

I heaved out a sigh, trying to let go of my anticipation for the trip.

"But I came up with a backup plan," Amber said.

I raised an eyebrow in question. With her bristly attitude, she didn't have a lot of school friends, and her mom claimed to be highly allergic. Our detective friend, Alex Martinez, worked twelve-hour days, plus he had a new police dog he was training, so he wasn't an option either.

"It turns out our hotel accepts pets." She continued to hide half her face behind Hunch, clearly concerned about my reaction.

"They accept pets? In the hotel rooms?"

Hearing the disbelief in my tone, Amber placed Hunch into the passenger seat and pulled out her phone. She navigated to the sponsoring hotel's website and flashed her screen to show me the words: AND YOU CAN BRING YOUR SMALL PET!

I stared at the words, tentatively allowing a spark of hope. "You want to bring Hunch on a fifteen-hour car ride?"

My eyebrow was so high, I was certain it blended with my hairline.

"Why not?" Spoken like a true teenager.

"Why not," I echoed under my breath. But I did have Hunch's litter box and food with me for Seth. Hunch knew better than to scratch up furniture. "You're going to be all by yourself for two days while we're on our food tour," I told my cat in my sternest tone.

This apparently signaled my agreement and made Amber squeal into the quiet early-morning air. She raced to the back of my car to throw her bag into the trunk.

I turned to my cat, who waited patiently on his haunches for Amber in the passenger seat with what could only be described as a look of triumph.

"You win," I told Hunch. "Apparently, you're coming with us."

Chapter Two

WITH ALMOST A THOUSAND miles to cover in one day, I didn't have much energy for arguing, so I caved pretty quickly to Amber's pleas to practice her driving. She needed fifty hours for her level one permit, and while her mom was getting better at communicating with her, she still didn't always keep up with the day-to-day needs of a teenager.

Soon, Amber had her phone hooked into the sound system, and music was playing. I was surprised it wasn't her usual top-forty fare.

"Jazz?" I asked.

"Uh-huh. I downloaded a whole playlist to get us in the mood."

Amber was like me that way. When she did things, she liked to do them right. With our latest venture—a catering business—she was forever coming up with theme ideas for our menus. "It'll make us memorable," she'd said right from the beginning. And it had. We had quickly gained a following within Honeysuckle Grove.

A road trip to New Orleans, followed up by an elite food tour, should have been exciting enough on its own to be memorable, but with the excitement in our lives lately, from helping our detective friend, Alex, in solving murder cases to quite literally running for our lives, I was happy to let Amber make these next four days memorable for less exciting reasons.

I was back in the driver's seat by the time we made it to our hotel, just after eleven, which was right downtown in the French Quarter and overlooked the Mississippi River. As expected for a Friday night, the city was lively with music and people, and if I hadn't been so exhausted, I might have wanted to go exploring.

"This is where they're putting us up?" Amber asked. "Ritzy."

High praise from a girl who had grown up traveling to five-star hotels with her family.

I felt a little underdressed in jeans and a T-shirt. After I parked, she grabbed her duffel bag from the trunk. I looked from my now-wide-awake cat to the tall tower of hotel rooms, lit along the frame with narrow blue lights.

"You're sure they allow pets?" I suddenly wondered if Amber had stretched the truth or shown me a different hotel's website in order to get her way.

Amber furrowed her brow, which didn't inspire confidence. "Oh. Yeah. Maybe I'll wait out here with Hunch while you double-check."

"They don't allow pets?" After a fifteen-hour drive, I was way too tired for this.

"They have some rooms for pets. Ask if they can move us to one." Amber shrugged, like this wasn't such a big deal.

I sighed out my fatigue and reached for the door.

I had a feeling it wasn't going to be that easy.

Chapter Three

SURE ENOUGH, THE FRONT desk clerk practically laughed in my face when I asked if my room allowed pets or if they could move me to a room that did.

The fortysomething man shook his head. "We have one theme room designed for small pets but it's always booked up months in advance. Why? You don't have a pet with you now?" The alarm was clear in his tone.

"Oh, no, nothing like that." I laughed nervously while wondering when I might have time to find us another pet-friendly hotel. "My niece was thinking of adopting a... dog while we're here in town. But I'll tell her it won't work this trip."

Thankfully, the front desk clerk accepted my explanation and handed over two key cards. I took them and gritted my teeth all the way to the car.

"Nope. No pets in our room," I told Amber the second she got out of the car. "Apparently, there's only one room allowing pets and it books up months in advance. Who knew?" Amber loved to dish out sarcasm, so I figured she'd better be able to take it.

She nodded, solemn for only about two seconds. Then she reached inside the car and retrieved Hunch, placing him into her duffel bag.

I pulled my small suitcase from the trunk, which had doubled in weight.

"What on earth...?"

"I put some of my stuff in there to make room for Hunch." Amber bent to murmur something to Hunch before covering the opening of the duffel bag with her jacket.

I supposed I should just be happy she had some kind of a plan. My tired brain was ready for a good night's sleep.

Inside the hotel's front doors, we angled for the elevator, but halfway through the small lobby, a tall slender blond man intercepted us.

"Mallory Beck?" he said such a strong Irish accent, it almost sounded put on. I nodded. "That's right."

"Howya? Liam O'Conner, at your service. I'll be your host from Foodie Elite Tour." He held out a hand, and I shook it. "Jerome said you'd pulled up." Liam motioned to the front desk clerk, who was watching us.

On instinct, I angled my body to hide Amber and her duffel bag. "Oh, yes. We couldn't leave West Virginia any earlier, so I'm afraid it was a long day of driving for us." I hoped he'd infer that all I wanted in the world right now was a bed.

But he just laughed heartily. "It's grand. And who's this youngwan with ya?"

I'd been trying to keep the focus away from Amber, so I quickly rattled off, "This is my niece, Amber. Hey, that's a great accent you have. Is it Irish?"

He nodded, but didn't elaborate. "And will you be joining us on the food tour, Amber?"

"Yeah, we're super excited for it, right, Aunt Mallory?" She elbowed me. We often posed as aunt and niece while working investigations, but I'd just saddled her with calling me Aunt Mallory for the duration of the two-day tour.

Liam turned toward the bar, which gave me a chance to sidestep a couple of feet away and press the elevator button. But when I turned back, another couple headed our way. "You should meet some of our other guests. We were chatting in the bar. Will you have a mineral with us?"

Was mineral water common in New Orleans? Or perhaps Ireland? Or was it code for some other sort of drink? Either way, I certainly didn't have the energy or the pet-freeness to sit and visit in a bar right now.

"Oh, I'd like to, but—"

"Clive, Scarlett, this here's Mallory and her niece, Amber. They'll be joining us on the tour."

Clive had a sweep of black bangs that appeared shellacked into place. He reached to shake my hand vigorously. "How y'all doin'? Nice of you to bring your niece to this thing. She's gonna learn a lot from me about good food. So are you, I bet." Clive's voice was even louder than Liam's, and I wondered how many "minerals" he'd had tonight.

Scarlett stood back and smiled quietly. She had bright orangey-red hair and wore a flowered tea-length swing dress, like something out of the fifties. I was about to ask about her gorgeous vintage pendant with tiny pearls draped along the bottom edge when she put in, "Clive knows a lot about food. He studied cooking in Paris."

"That's right." Clive puffed out his chest.

I hadn't been to Paris, but from everything I'd heard, I had trouble envisioning loudmouthed immodest Clive studying there.

"Come on! Join us in the bar," Clive said. "Liam's been rattling on about himself for too long."

I had a feeling Clive had been the self-involved talker.

"Ahh, Mallory and Amber are knackered," Liam answered for me. "And I should get some good sleep myself. Going to be a full day tomorrow."

Clive's eyes slid down to Amber's side, where she clutched her duffel.

I stepped into his vision and reached out a hand. "It was so nice to meet you, Clive. I look forward to getting to know you and Scarlett better in the morning."

Thankfully, the three of them let us go. As I looked at Amber's slightly wriggling duffel bag, I wondered if Liam was also staying in the hotel and if he'd be joining us in the elevator. But thankfully, a second later, the elevator dinged its arrival, and Liam stuck around to wish Clive and Scarlett a good night.

"What are we going to do with Hunch while we're on tour?" We walked down the third-floor hallway and I slid my key card into the lock of a fancily carved white door. "If we leave him here, the maid will find him."

As I opened the door, Amber pulled the Do Not Disturb sign from the back of it. "We'll just put this up."

Everything seemed so easy for Amber.

"There's no way his litter pan will fit in either your duffel bag or my suitcase. How do you suppose we're going to sneak that up here?" I hoped she had let my cat out on some grass before bringing him upstairs.

She shrugged—her ever-present response to every conundrum. "So we'll bring him in the car."

"In the middle of July?"

"We'll put the sign up, and I'll come back and take him out." She swept by me into our room and effectively changed the subject. "Whoa, Mallory! Look at this room."

She placed her duffel bag on the floor, and Hunch wormed his way out of it. A second later, he was sniffing every inch of our floor in dog-like fashion.

The Mardi Gras-themed room was decked out in lime green and fuchsia drapes. At the end of our brocaded bedspreads was a row of brightly colored bobbles the size of my head that imitated Mardi Gras beads.

"This is awesome!" Amber spun around and landed on her back on one of the beds, looking up at the chandelier and the masks that decorated the upper half of the room.

It warmed my heart to see her this happy. I didn't think I'd heard her so excited in the entire year I'd known her. And I decided right then that at sixteen, she deserved some wonder in her life.

I sighed and dropped onto the other bed.

We'd figure out what to do with Hunch after a good night's sleep. Instead of focusing on what was wrong, I turned to Amber, smiled, and said, "Yes, this is all going to be amazing."

Chapter Four

MORNING CAME TOO SOON.

"Shower's all yours," Amber said from her place in the middle of the hotel room floor. I blinked to clear my eyes. She had Hunch up on his hind paws and was looking him square in the eye. "Now you're going to be a good kitty and keep out of sight today, right, Hunchie?"

I pushed up in bed. "We probably need to take him out."

"Already did. By the way, the front desk clerks this morning aren't nearly as nosy as that guy last night. We shouldn't have any problem getting Hunch in and out today."

Shouldn't. But what if we did?

I looked at Hunch, who was staring back at Amber as though he truly understood every word that came out of her mouth. I made a noncommittal noise and headed for the shower.

Half an hour later, we made it to the lobby to find Liam chatting with a couple in their fifties. They had matching salt-and-pepper hair and stiff postures.

"Mallory, Amber! I'm glad you're ready to go. Come and meet Victor Kinsley and his wife, Victoria."

I chuckled as I reached out a hand. "Victor and Victoria, huh?"

Victor shook my hand, his face stoic. "That's right."

"We hear you're all the way from West Virginia, dear?" Victoria asked, shaking

Amber's hand.

I answered for both of us. "Yes. We got in late last night. Where are you folks from?"

"A couple hours upstate," Victoria told me. "Just outside Lafayette."

I'd never thought of West Virginia as being a long way from Louisiana, but so far, Amber and I felt like the outliers.

"We're looking forward to trying the New Orleans fare," I told them all. "Are you also a winner of the Foodie Elite Recipe Contest?"

Victor's snigger told me this he found amusing. "No. This tour costs a pretty penny for those who haven't won a contest, I can assure you."

Oh. I'd just assumed this would be a group of chefs or wannabe chefs who had all submitted award-winning original recipes. I looked over Victor and Victoria Kinsley a little closer, though.

Her diamond earrings and his tailored dress shirt suggested people of means. I suddenly felt a little underdressed in my peach and fuchsia flowered sundress. At least I'd talked Amber out of her usual sneakers and big-statement hoodies. Today, she wore a jean skirt with an off-the-shoulder cream flounce top that looked gorgeous with her auburn hair.

Just then, a woman in jeans and a pink T-shirt walked up. She had mousy brown hair and wore a bright shade of pink lipstick that matched her top. "Liam, right?"

Liam looked at a clipboard in his hands. "You must be Lisa Lorenson?"

Her ponytail bobbed as she nodded, and Liam made the introductions to the rest of us. At least I no longer felt underdressed.

"I'm so glad I made it on time! I was worried with traffic this morning!" Lisa continued to babble about the drive. If she and the Kinsleys had driven in this morning, did that mean none of them were contest winners and hadn't been treated to a room at this beautiful hotel?

"Are you from around here?" I asked when she finally stopped to take a breath.

"From Jackson," she told me, and then that launched her into another diatribe about the trucker that cut her off and how she'd spilled her coffee all over her car.

I still hadn't seen Clive and his girlfriend, Scarlett, from last night. Because they were at the bar until late, I had to assume they were also recipe award winners staying at the hotel. Studying in Paris couldn't have hurt.

I was about to ask after them when a man on a nearby velvet bench caught my attention. He looked over his newspaper at our group every few seconds.

The man must have also caught Liam's attention. He walked over and said, "You're not by chance Mr. Emile Dubois?"

He replied in a quiet French accent. "Oui, I am Monsieur Dubois."

"Oh, well, fine morning to ya!" Liam held out his hand. Monsieur Dubois looked at it for several seconds before standing to shake it. Emile Dubois wore jeans and a short-sleeve white T-shirt. I never would have guessed him for a Frenchman preparing to go on a food tour. I got the impression he would have sat there until we left the hotel, missing the tour altogether simply due to shyness. "Come! Join us!"

Monsieur Dubois obeyed, but remained silent as Liam introduced him. Relief crossed his face when Clive and

Scarlett stepped off the elevator, effectively snatching the attention away from him.

"We're not late, are we?" Clive checked the time on his phone. He wore a black dress shirt with a sheen and had three buttons undone, revealing the top of a hairy chest. I glanced at the lobby clock. It was ten after.

"Not a bit!" Liam said regardless. "Well, that's grand. We've got everyone together."

Clive's girlfriend, Scarlett, wore another fifties-style dress, this one yellow. It looked striking with her fiery hair. She wore the same vintage pendant, but today, the brass buttons on her dress also had a vintage look, with ornate circles around the outside and a leaping dog in the center of each one. I wondered if she had a dog. Then I wondered what I would look like in a dress with cat buttons.

But did I really want my appearance to scream cat lady?

"Where did you get that beautiful pendant?" I asked to get that thought out of my head.

She fingered it. "Oh, at an antique store in town. I work in a local museum, so I'm always on the lookout for beautiful old trinkets. Did you see the one I found for Clive?"

I didn't particularly want to look at her boyfriend's bare chest. The round pendant he wore also looked antique, though not my style. It contained a large blue stone with a black dot in the middle, making it look like someone's eye.

I forced a smile and nodded.

Liam clapped his hands. "Our first stop is the Maison de Tarte."

"House of pies?" Amber murmured to me, her tone excited. "We're starting with pie?"

"I know the one," Clive said. "I'll tell y'all exactly what to order."

Liam cleared his throat. "Actually, we have a special menu we'll be ordering from today." Clive seemed put off by this information and gave Scarlett a raised eyebrow look. Liam ignored this and went on. "It's right here in the French Quarter, only a wee saunter from here." Liam motioned toward the door.

"Oh, um, I have to run upstairs," I said. They all looked at me, so I felt the need to explain and figured I might as well be honest. I dropped my voice, even though we were too far from the front desk for any hotel employees to hear. "You see, I have my cat along and I should just check on him before we head out."

Clive balked. "People are too attached to their pets. Can't leave them be for five minutes." His words were so loud, my cheeks warmed.

"I should grab my sweater from upstairs." Amber pulled me toward the elevator. "Maison de Tarte. We'll meet you there."

Liam looked confused by our straying from the plan, but only for a second. Then he led the way toward the doors with the rest of the group following him. Emile trailed at a distance, and I wondered if he was considering ditching the tour altogether. With Clive Richards as one of his companions, it wouldn't surprise me if the shy Frenchman didn't even make it to the first stop.

Chapter Five

I STAGGERED OUT OF Maison de Tarte an hour later, delighted with the beignet I had chosen at Monsieur Dubois's suggestion. The pastry was about the only memorable item, though. The rest of the food had been fairly ordinary, nothing special, and Clive's know-it-all brashness was casting a pall on the group. Victoria's food intolerances had provided another wrinkle—it seemed she couldn't have anything with dairy, gluten, or egg, which made me wonder why she had chosen to come on this tour in the first place.

Liam's smile was starting to fray at the edges, and I didn't blame him. Still, with effort, he kept it in place and gave us an overview of some of New Orleans's attractions as we walked toward our second stop. Amber had raced back to the hotel to check in on Hunch, promising she'd be more than capable of finding the next restaurant on her own.

"Are you from the area?" I asked Monsieur Dubois as I walked at the rear of the group with him. He'd recommended the beignet, after all, calling it, "Very French. Very New Orleans."

He shrugged with one shoulder. "Originally, non. Originally from a small village in Bordeaux. But now, oui. I own a restaurant in the city."

"You own a restaurant here in New Orleans?" I didn't realize how loud I'd been until Clive looked back from where he walked alongside Liam, adding his two cents to Liam's description of the local sights.

Monsieur Dubois dipped his gaze to the sidewalk in front of him. "Just a small place."

I lowered my voice. I was too curious not to ask more, even if Monsieur Dubois was normally too shy to talk about himself. "What kind of food do you serve at your restaurant?" If the restaurants on this tour didn't improve, I'd much rather garner an invitation to his establishment.

He smiled meekly. "It is a mix of French and seafood, with a soupçon of Cajun."

"Sounds delicious. We'd love to stop by before we leave town. What is it called?" I pulled out my phone, but when I looked up with it, poised and ready, Monsieur Dubois had locked eyes with Clive. Liam continued on, now talking about a nearby museum we should visit, but Clive had stopped in place to glare back at the Frenchman. A strange tension stretched between them, and I wondered what I'd missed.

"You don't have anything to add, Clive?" Liam asked in what seemed like a dig, but Clive didn't take it that way.

"Newcomb Art Museum is the best in the city." Clive puffed out his chest, as though he had curated the place. "Scarlett can get you a discount, can't you, Scarlett?" Clive sidled up beside his girlfriend and pawed at her purse. "Give them a discount card."

She dug into her purse, but kept her face downturned as she said, "Oh, um, actually, hon, my discount only works at some of the smaller museums."

A long pause followed, but then thankfully, Liam took over, directing our attention to a nearby park worth visiting. The rest of us kept moving, but Clive and Scarlett were at a standstill.

"I guess you're not as important as you try to make out." As we passed, he gritted out, "How could you embarrass me like that? You made me look like a fool."

A moment later, she caught up with the rest of us, avoiding Clive's eyes as she passed a business card to each of us. "The discounted museums are listed on the back. You'll get twenty percent off, but I'm afraid I can't help with the bigger museums."

I barely had time to skim the list of six museums when Clive made his way up to the front of the group beside Liam again and interrupted my thoughts with his loud voice.

"I just think if you're looking for culture, you go on one of the local cultural tours. We're looking for the best food in New Orleans."

I hated to admit it, but I agreed with Clive. Liam smiled in Clive's direction with a close-lipped smile, one that looked fake even from my distance. "We at Foodie Elite provide access to a wide array of the best cuisine in New Orleans." Liam's usually lighthearted Irish accent sounded strained with a seemingly prepared script. He clapped his hands, but everything about the motion seemed forced. "Don't you worry. We're almost at our next stop."

But Clive didn't let up in trying to convince Liam to change some of the stops on the tour. He pointed behind us and listed the names of three other restaurants he felt were worth visiting. I wasn't sure if I believed much of what Clive said, but I made a mental note of the names just the same.

Liam's voice tightened even more as he pointed us forward. "Like I said. Almost there."

At least the tour wouldn't be boring. I wondered if we'd get through the entire two-day food tour without our host throttling his most irritating attendee.

Chapter Six

THE NEXT STOP DIDN'T inspire much confidence.

Donnie's Irish Pub.

As abrasive as Clive Richards was, he might also be right. Were we simply on a cash-grab food tour that offered stops at a handful of local joints that needed some extra publicity?

I gnawed on my lip as I waited for Amber under the green neon sign. It didn't take long. In fact, with the colorful people I'd been grouped with, I'd barely had time to worry about the teenager I'd brought into this big city being on her own before she reappeared. Her relaxed smile disarmed me as she strode up. In truth, Amber had navigated our way from West Virginia to our hotel room, thanks to the GPS on her phone, but she was still much more efficient at it than I was.

After she told me how much Hunch was enjoying his holiday, we walked through the front door of Donnie's, but as soon as the jiggy Irish music hit my ears, I asked Amber, "What kind of a New Orleans food tour starts at an Irish pub?"

She shrugged, smiling. "I dunno. A fun one?"

I raised my eyebrows at her attempt to groove to the music as she made her way through the busy pub toward a weathered bar, where the rest of our group sat.

Monsieur Dubois caught my attention, standing not too far from the bar, looking at Donnie's pub merchandise. This was getting more commercial by the minute. But I headed there anyway. Of anything on this tour, I was enjoying Monsieur Dubois's company and insight the most.

"See anything you like?" I sidled up beside him and surveyed the black and green T-shirts and beer mugs on display.

"Shall we sit?" Monsieur Dubois motioned toward the bar. As at Maison de Tarte, Liam sat at the far end with Clive, whether or not Liam liked it. I could already hear them arguing over the loud music. Clive argued about how Kerry or Finnegan's would've made a better choice for the tour.

"I don't know why we have to have a stop at an Irish pub at all," I murmured to Monsieur Dubois as he took the barstool beside me.

Amber was chatting with Clive's girlfriend and smiled brightly. Amber didn't have any interest in alcohol, as her dad hadn't been a great drinking example. I was glad she was having fun, and Scarlett seemed the closest to her age out of anyone in the group.

"The Irish community in New Orleans is not so terrible," Monsieur Dubois said, surprising me. I would have expected a French restaurateur to have more refined taste. But when he went on, I wondered if I was missing something. "The places you least expect often have their spécialités. If you come to New Orleans for only one day, you miss so much. There is variety and richness, if only one takes the time."

"Hmm. So do you agree with Clive Richards that there are better Irish pubs in town?"

Monsieur Dubois's lip curled up on one side. "I do not agree with that man about anything."

I was taken aback by the venom in Monsieur Dubois's words.

The bartender approached to take orders. I hadn't even seen a menu yet.

But apparently, Monsieur Dubois knew what he wanted. "Smithwick's if you have?"

The bartender chuckled. "Always." He leaned in closer to me and asked in a voice filled with natural hills and valleys, "And what can I get for the lady?"

I was surprised when Monsieur Dubois answered for me. "The mademoiselle is looking to experience New Orleans food and drink for the first time."

The bartender held up his fingers in the shape of a pretend gun toward Monsieur Dubois. "Gotcha." He moved along to Lisa, who giggled at whatever the Irish bartender said to her.

I was more concerned with whatever Monsieur Dubois had just ordered for me. "You know, I am pretty picky." This wasn't completely true. I enjoyed ninety percent of most food and drinks if they were prepared well. But it was about the anticipation. And perhaps a little about keeping control.

Monsieur Dubois didn't reply, which only made my control issues flare harder. He raised an eyebrow and nodded.

The bartender moved onto Mr. and Mrs. Kinsley, and an argument developed.

"Look at the assortment, darling," Victor said to his wife. "You have to grant me one beer."

"But the wheat!" Victoria said the words to the bartender, but they were directed at her husband.

"Ah, we have a great variety of barley beer. Do you like a good lager?" His fun-loving tone hadn't changed as he directed his question at Victor, but Victoria stood from her barstool, huffed, and pulled her arms across her chest. Her stool, now that I could see it, was in the shape of a horse's rear.

"We don't drink beer," she said.

"Honey..." Victor's tone with his wife seemed meek. "I'm not sensitive to—"

"But solidarity!" she hissed. "You promised."

The bartender didn't miss a beat, listing off beer and lager varieties with a barley base. His natural accent made me question again if Liam might be putting his on or, at the very least, enhancing it.

The bartender's smooth tongue didn't lighten Victoria Kinsley's concerns, though, and a second later, Clive arrived behind them and clapped a hand on each of their backs.

"Let the dude have what he likes to drink," he told Victoria, his voice more commanding than jovial. He turned to Victor. "She doesn't own ya, does she?"

Victoria's eyes widened, and she spun away from Clive to get his hand off her.

"If you ask me, this world is about natural selection, survival of the fittest. People who can't handle a little gluten, are they really going to last? Why should they be around taking up all the resources of the planet?" Clive let out a hearty laugh, as though he hadn't just told Victoria she might as well die.

"Nobody's asking you," Victor gritted out. Everyone at the bar had gone silent, making the jovial Irish music seem suddenly out of place. Scarlett popped out of her chair, raced over to Clive, and whispered something the rest of us couldn't hear.

He didn't take the time to listen to her and instead wrapped a possessive arm around her shoulder. "People should learn to take a joke." He let out another loud guffaw.

Victoria looked at her husband, but when he didn't open his mouth to stand up to Clive, she turned and marched straight for the ladies' room near the back of the bar with tears in her eyes.

Victor watched his wife go and then turned to Clive. "We can order for ourselves, thank you very much."

Scarlett's cheeks were bright pink. Clive held her close. He opened his mouth to say more, but Victor simply held up a finger toward him and said, "Ah—Ah—" When Clive finally closed his mouth, Victor went on in a low, angry tone. "My wife suffers from serious depression, brought on by certain foods and life situations. I'll ask you to keep your distance for the rest of the tour."

Clive's scoff was quieter than his earlier outbursts, but he repeated Victor's words, "I'll ask you to keep your distance," in a mocking tone on the way back to his stool.

Victor ordered a water. Liam, it seemed, didn't feel Clive Richards was worth arguing with, even if his abrasive attitude was wreaking havoc on the tour, and popped out of his own stool to have a conversation with the bartender.

Victoria stayed in the bathroom for so long that a drink and a platter of appetizers landed in front of me on the bar.

Amber already had a drink in her hand, but I didn't notice until Clive said loud enough for us all to hear, "How old are you? Are you even allowed to be in here?"

Amber's response couldn't be heard at our end of the bar. She vacated her seat beside Scarlett to come and see what had arrived at our end.

"What are you having?" I asked at the same time she asked the same thing of me. I shrugged. "Actually, I have no idea. The bartender and Monsieur Dubois cooked up some sort of order for me." Now that it had arrived, my control issues subsided. This seemed fun.

"I'm having a virgin mango margarita," Amber told me, offering me a sip of her layered orange drink. I shook my head. I'd try some later, but I wanted to keep my palette clear for what had been chosen for me.

A platter filled with what looked like hot peppers arrived down the bar in front of Clive. Little tent cards with numbers sat among the peppers, reminding me of the markers used at crime scenes.

"Liam's in for the challenge, right, mate?" Clive bellowed, badly imitating his accent. "Who else?"

"They're having a pepper eating contest," Amber explained. "Apparently, it's a regular thing at this pub."

I raised an eyebrow. "And you're not interested?"

She shook her head. "Not with him. He's like a child who can't get enough good attention, so he'll try for any kind of attention."

It surprised me when Monsieur Dubois stood from his stool. "You may count me in." His voice was self-assured enough that we could all hear it. Two other gentlemen at a nearby table also volunteered to take part.

"This should be fun." I elbowed Amber.

Most of the food on the platter before me was deep-fried, and I could only recognize the shape of the zucchini wedges. Everything else was a mystery. My golden drink was in a short heavy glass, with a floating mint leaf.

"A mint julep?" I asked the bartender. I had read up on Louisiana cuisine and knew the drink only by name. I'd never tasted one.

The bartender winked at me. "Donnie's Irish Mint Julep. Taste it. It has our special twist."

I took a small sip and then a bigger one. It wasn't my favorite mix of flavors, but still so unique I had to figure out the possible ingredients. "What's your special twist?"

The bartender only winked again and then moved down the bar to pick up discarded napkins as Clive and his competitors had consumed their first peppers seemingly without any pain or suffering.

"I bet that's a fried pickle." Amber pointed to something on my platter. Fried pickles were popular in West Virginia. However, I could only see their appeal when served with an appropriate entrée, not so much as an appetizer on their own.

"Go ahead," I told her. "Try it and tell me."

Amber slid onto Monsieur Dubois's empty stool. She took a bite of pickle, and her eyes widened. "You have to try this, Mallory."

"Why? Is it spicy?"

"There's something in the batter." She cut a small slice. "See if you can figure out what it is."

While I chewed and considered, the bartender returned and answered my unasked question. "That's buttermilk you're tastin'. Nice, yes?"

Amber nodded hyperactively. "Nice!"

She sliced and divided the rest of the appetizers. This was normally my job, but I was so intrigued with my mystery mint julep, I sipped at it in an effort to place the ingredients.

The pepper competitors moved onto their next heat challenge. Some hand-waving in front of mouths and quick drinking followed.

"I told you to order milk," Clive gritted out toward Scarlett, loud enough that the whole bar could probably hear. She lowered her head. Clive spoke quieter to her, and his contorted face told me they were angry words. A second later, she jumped up from her stool and ran for the ladies' room, covering her face. That was becoming a habit with the women in our group.

"See? He's a child." Amber raised her eyebrows and speared another chunk of deep-fried mystery food. "Okra?" she guessed, passing a speared chunk to me. I took it, glad she was along to help me eat all this fried food. If not for her, I would be rolling down Bourbon Street by the end of this tour.

I agreed it was okra, pleasantly surprised that Amber could place it, and she went on to tell me about the conversation she'd had with Scarlett.

"She works right here in the French Quarter and says it's a lot of fun living in the city."

"A lot of fun, even with that boyfriend?" I chuckled under my breath.

"Yeah, no kidding. He's critical of everything she says and everything she orders." Amber shook her head. "I suppose being a food critic is the perfect job for Clive Richards."

Just as she said his name, Clive threw up his hands, perturbed, and said, "I'm out," clearly hating to lose. "But you guys have to endure the next round to be declared the winners." His words sounded like a threat.

Liam chuckled. "I'm afraid I'm out, too." He wiped his mouth with a napkin and took a big swig of his highball drink. The two other bar patrons also held up their hands and backed away.

Everyone looked to Monsieur Dubois, expecting his forfeit, but he popped the final hot pepper, a bright reddish-orange one, into his mouth. He stared at Clive Richards as he chewed and then swallowed, not even relieving the sting with a mouthful of water.

"We have another Donnie's Pepper Champion, ladies and gentlemen!" The bartender offered a black and green T-shirt to Monsieur Dubois, and all the people in the bar erupted in applause. Amber and I joined them.

"I must excuse myself," Monsieur Dubois said and headed for the restrooms. Whether he was bothered by the heat or not, he kept his composure until he was out of sight.

I looked at Amber, her last words sitting with me. "Is Clive Richards really a food critic?"

She nodded. Monsieur Dubois had a clear dislike for the man, but I'd thought it had been a simple personality clash. I wondered if Clive had actually given Monsieur Dubois's restaurant a poor review.

Scarlett returned from the restroom with a forced smile and watery eyes. She remained standing to finish her drink, not getting close enough to Clive that he could blame her for his recent loss. A second later, he stood and beckoned the bartender to the wall of T-shirts.

"That Dubois character cheated!" Clive's words were whispered, but even his whispers were louder than the average speaking voice. He pulled out some cash, but the bartender shook his head.

Apparently, Donnie's Irish Pub T-shirts weren't for sale, even in the event of an unfair loss. They could only be won.

I had barely turned back to Amber when Liam O'Conner popped off his barstool and clapped his hands. "It's time to move onto our next stop, ladies and gents." His tight smile made me wonder if we were cutting this stop short due to Clive's abrasiveness.

Everyone downed their drinks, gathered their things, and headed for the door. Amber had been snapping photos since arriving in New Orleans and pulled out her phone to get a snapshot of the antique bar. I took an extra second to try the rest of the items on my platter, and Clive must have still felt the heat from the peppers because he knocked back two more cocktails and a glass of water before heading for the door. By the time we made it outside, Monsieur Dubois had reappeared, looking composed, and Liam explained the directions to the next stop on our food tour. Clive and Scarlett stood a few feet down the sidewalk, arguing.

"We've barely started the tour!" he hissed.

"I have to work. I told you that." Scarlett stepped away, but he grabbed for her hand to tether her back.

Scarlett tried to yank her hand away, but Clive held it firmly.

Before I knew what was happening, Amber approached the arguing couple. "Have a great day at work!" she told Scarlett, narrowing her eyes at Clive.

This wasn't the first time Amber had acted impulsively, leaving me imagining a hundred awful repercussions. But a moment later, Scarlett snatched her hand away, skirted around the group, and said, "Bye, everybody!" in a too-bright tone. "I'll see you at the first stop tomorrow!"

As I watched her go, I couldn't help but think that if I had a boyfriend like Clive, I'd make up any excuse to get away from him.

Chapter Seven

AS TASTY AS THE appetizers had been, I hoped Liam's Irish influence didn't mean we'd spend our entire two days in New Orleans at Irish pubs. It worried me even more when Clive sidled up to Lisa and expressed the same concern.

"I'm sure Liam knows what he's doing," Lisa argued from in front of Amber and me. Liam was at the front of our pack, trying to smooth things over with the Kinsleys, and Clive, this one time, seemed to take the hint and had fallen behind.

Although, the more he spoke, the more I wondered if he had only fallen back to stir up some gossip. "That guy is choosing ridiculous places. If you ask me, he's taking bribes from these restaurants, trying to get a little kickback. Maybe I'll call the magazine, get the guy fired."

With Clive's bluster, he neglected to notice that Liam had stopped up ahead to speak about a statue on the corner. By Liam's wide eyes and stark expression, I guessed he'd heard that last bit of Clive's plans.

"Maybe we should check on Hunch?" I suggested to Amber, mostly to break the strange silence, but she said she wanted to order first.

This third restaurant wasn't far, but apparently, it was hard to find. As soon as Liam regained his composure, he said, "This is the statue you'll want to look for if you're coming back, as the alley is unmarked."

Amber touched the trombone on the bronze jazz player and then snapped a photo of it. Someone had strung purple, gold, and green Mardi Gras beads around his neck.

We made our way around the statue and into a nearly deserted alley. There were no signs down the alleyway at all.

Thirty feet along, Liam found a cedar door with a black iron handle. It made me nervous, taking a sixteen-year-old girl through an unmarked door down a deserted back alley, but once Liam had the door held open for us, the joyful cacophony from inside had me feeling more at ease.

There had to be fifty people crammed into the small restaurant, all talking loudly to be heard over the big band music playing through overhead speakers. Even with dim lighting, it was easy to find the large empty table with a reserved sign in the middle of the room.

Soon, Liam stood at the end of our oblong wood table, offering a speech on the history of the local cuisine served here at Café Ennoe.

Amber and I slipped silently into two chairs at the opposite end of the table.

"Anyone of you not tried a po' boy yet?" Liam surveyed the table, where Amber and I were the only two raising our hands.

I knew a po' boy was a sandwich with deep-fried fish at its center. As appealing as that might have been any other day, and as happy as I was to finally have landed at a restaurant with some local cuisine, I had just wolfed down an array of deep-fried hors d'ouevres and could do with something lighter.

"The po' boy, originally called the poor boy, is a sandwich developed by the Martin brothers, right here in the heart of New Orleans. The Martin brothers ran the streetcars, and during the strike of 1929, they created a special sandwich to feed their fellow out-of-work operators."

As Liam went on, I sighed, knowing I absolutely would be trying a po' boy. I was a sucker for any food that had a story behind it.

"Café Ennoe serves the best po' boy in town, hands down."

Clive scoffed at this sentiment. He leaned into Lisa and whispered something. She pulled away, but the man with few boundaries didn't notice and only leaned closer.

Liam went on, pointedly keeping his gaze from Clive. "I suggest the original oyster loaf if you're lookin' for something steeped in culture."

At this, Clive turned up his nose and jabbered on to the rest of the table with his plethora of opinions on the subject. "The oyster loaf is the only one I wouldn't get. Go for the fried shrimp or crawfish. Trust me." He leaned back and crossed his arms.

Our waitress arrived and passed out a string of Mardi Gras beads to each of us as she circled our table. All the wait staff wore cream blouses with black skirts and burgundy aprons. Our waitress had bronze skin and dark hair. Her name tag read: JULIANA. Her strong French accent elevated the choices. "Our most popular po' boy are the oyster, fried shrimp, fried crawfish, fried catfish, and Louisiana hot sausage. Some of our less common varieties are French fries, fried chicken, duck, and rabbit. We also have a sampler po' boy platter, where you may choose three kinds."

Amber and I knew what we would be ordering. Now it was just a matter of choosing our six varieties.

Our waitress stopped as she made it to Clive, but then took a sudden step away, pointing at his neck. Her eyes widened, and she said, "Maudeet!"

"What?" He touched the antique eye-like charm.

"You must take that off in here!"

Her tone was grave, but Clive only raised an eyebrow and chuckled. "You can't tell me what to do, honey. My girlfriend gave this to me. Besides, it's antique."

The waitress outstretched a strand of purple Mardi Gras beads toward him, but didn't step any closer. As she turned to walk away, she balled her fists and muttered, "Mort," which I recognized, even though I'd never taken French. My French teacher in culinary arts school used to flap his hands up and use that word whenever a dish was past its prime and no longer servable. It meant dead.

The waitress rushed off for more beads, but this was the opening Victoria had been waiting for to send a jab in Clive's direction.

"Where did your date go, again?" Victoria sneered at Clive. He looked stunned and then angered by the question.

I avoided the tension by turning to Monsieur Dubois. "Have you had a po' boy from here before?"

He raised his eyebrows. "At Café New Orleans? Ah, but of course."

Clive stood, slapped his Mardi Gras beads down on the table, and bellowed loud enough for all of us to hear, "Get me a shrimp po' boy. I'm getting some air." He knocked our chairs as he pushed past us, and I wondered how many drinks he'd guzzled back in our short time at Donnie's Irish Pub.

I turned my attention back to Monsieur Dubois. "Café New Orleans? Is that an affectionate term from the locals for Café Ennoe?"

Monsieur Dubois smirked but didn't answer, and my mind turned over, wondering what I was missing. Then it hit me. With no signage, I'd only ever heard Café Ennoe spoken. "Is it spelled Café N.O.?"

Monsieur Dubois nodded once, chuckling.

"What kind do you suggest? Have you tried the oyster loaf that Liam suggested?"

Monsieur Dubois shrugged one shoulder. "Oyster loaf is fine. I enjoy catfish or Louisiana hot sausage the best."

I nodded, and when Juliana made it around to me, I ordered those three varieties, while Amber chose French fries, fried chicken, and duck.

Monsieur Dubois ordered a ham po' boy, which hadn't been on the list and definitely hadn't been listed among his favorites. As soon as the waitress gave him a green strand of Mardi Gras beads and moved on to the Kinsleys and their long list of food requirements, Monsieur Dubois explained without me having to pry.

"I must always try new flavors when I visit the local eateries."

That made sense. As much as I didn't want to stir up any agitation, I wanted to ask about his restaurant before Clive returned. "Have you ever run into Mr. Richards professionally?"

Monsieur Dubois cleared his throat and looked down, clearly uncomfortable. Maybe it made Amber uncomfortable as well because she popped out of her chair.

"I'm going to run back and check on Hunch."

As she left, Monsieur Dubois asked, "What is a hunch?"

I smiled at his attempt to change the subject. I had been in the investigation business for too long to get diverted that easily. "Hunch is my cat. Unfortunately, my cat-sitter ducked out at the last minute, so he's along for the ride. But you were about to tell me about Clive Richards?"

"Po' boy would be a good name for Monsieur Richards. He visited my restaurant as a food critic only one time and he walked out without a payment!" Monsieur Dubois's eyes flared, the liveliest and most emotional I'd seen him. "He threatened if I didn't compensate the bill, he would write a scathing review."

"And he left a bad review?" It sounded as though Monsieur Dubois didn't have a choice about comping the meal.

Before I could ask more, Monsieur Dubois stood from his chair. "Please excuse me." He headed for the restrooms near the door, but I suspected he was only trying to escape my questions.

While he was gone, I reprimanded myself. Why did I always have to nose into everyone's business?

Our table was nearly empty. Lisa sat a few seats away, tapping into her phone. Liam had accompanied the Kinsleys to the kitchen to speak with the chef. A place that specialized in sandwiches and deep-fried items may not offer the best workarounds for someone like Victoria Kinsley.

A back alley place like this would have an interesting kitchen, though. Would it be too strange for me to suddenly develop a food issue I simply had to discuss with the chef?

As I played this out in my mind, I didn't notice Lisa finish up on her phone until she slid into Amber's chair beside me.

"Clive said he's going to call the magazine and get Liam fired." When she leaned in to whisper this, she reminded me of Donna Mayberry from church, our town gossip back in Honeysuckle Grove.

"He thinks Liam's taking bribes?" I guessed, remembering the statement Clive had made on the walk here.

"He was going to go outside and call the first two restaurants to confirm it. I went out with a guy like him once. If you ask me, he just likes to stir up trouble."

I couldn't disagree with that sentiment. He'd even tried to make a fuss over Amber not being old enough to be in the Irish pub.

She huffed. "Someone like him shouldn't even be allowed on a food tour."

I nodded, even though her opinion was a little extreme.

"Did you hear what he said to Mrs. Kinsley at the Irish pub?" She went on without waiting for my answer. "He said he was a big believer in natural selection. Only the strongest of us should survive and use up the resources on this planet." Lisa threw up her hands. "None of us could believe it. I mean, he was basically saying that if Victoria can't handle a little gluten, she might as well be dead!"

"Yes, that was certainly out of place." I glanced around for Juliana, needing a refill on my water, as this conversation was making me parched. I couldn't see her anywhere.

What a crazy group of people we'd been slotted to spend two days with. It was amazing they hadn't all killed each other.

That was my last thought before the door swung open, and a pale-faced Amber stood in the doorway. Her stunned energy quieted the place.

"Mallory, come quick! Mr. Richards is collapsed in the alley."

Chapter Eight

I RACED OUT THE door with my phone already at my ear. When the 911 operator answered, I gave her a play-by-play.

"There's an unconscious man in an alley in the French Quarter." I surveyed the gathering crowd, most from within the restaurant, and begged for help with an address. I sputtered it off as our waitress recited it. "He's facedown, and he isn't responding to his name. Clive Richards," I told the operator when she asked. "Should I check for a pulse?" The operator only instructed me not to move him.

I decided to take this as permission and bent to feel Clive's cold and clammy wrist. No pulse at all. I reached for his neck and saw a green string of Mardi Gras beads beneath his overturned body. He'd been given a string of purple beads. I was sure of it. These weren't around his neck, though, but were doubled and lying on the ground beneath him. Looking closer, I saw impressions of the beads along the side of his neck. Avoiding the impressions, I checked for a pulse, but found nothing.

Had Clive Richards been strangled to death?

After relaying the details to the 911 operator, I hung up and called to the growing crowd, "An ambulance is on its way. We've been instructed not to move this man."

"When I left, he was pacing and yelling into his phone." Amber sidled up beside me. She had Hunch on his leash, which he had little patience for under normal circumstances. Now, with a murder afoot, he pulled toward Clive's body like a dog straining for a meat-encased bone. "I came back and he was like this. Hunch really wants to have a sniff?" She asked it as a question.

I doubted, after my recent instruction, the crowd would overlook a cat sniffing around a dead body, so I murmured to her, "Just a little closer, under the pretense of keeping everyone back."

"All right, people." She didn't need any more instruction. "Let's give the man some room and make way for the ambulance to get through as soon as it gets here."

The crowd shuffled and murmured to each other. Amber used this opportunity to circle the body, with Hunch leading the way. As soon as I got Hunch away from public scrutiny, I'd be sure to explain my suspicion of strangulation.

While Amber played her part, I played mine, surveying the crowd for anyone who had known Clive Richards. As I found each person from our table around the perimeter, looking on with interest, it occurred to me that each one had some heated feelings against Clive. Each one was a suspect.

Liam O'Conner, who had been clearly frustrated by having Clive on the tour and had heard Clive threaten to get him fired on the way here.

Victor and Victoria Kinsley, who Clive had offended at the Irish pub. Not to mention he may have sent Victoria into a depressive spiral.

Lisa Lorenson, who had clearly wanted Clive off the tour altogether.

And Emile Dubois, who had a grudge against the food critic who had left a scathing review of his restaurant.

Even our waitress had had an abrasive reaction to Clive or, at least, to his antique choker. I walked around his body to see his neck again. Sure enough, the choker was no longer on him.

I looked around for Julianna, our waitress, but all of the wait staff seemed to have gone back inside.

The only person whose presence I could account for at the time of Clive's death was Lisa's, as she had been sitting at the table with me the entire time. Clive had embarrassed Amber, too, and even her presence was unaccounted for.

A sick feeling filled my stomach as I envisioned having to stay in New Orleans to prove Amber's innocence.

Chapter Nine

I FINGERED THE PURPLE strand of beads around my neck as the ambulance siren grew closer.

Mrs. Kinsley's beads were also purple. Mr. Kinsley and Liam both wore yellow-gold strands of beads that were still around their necks. Monsieur Dubois had definitely been given a green strand, but he no longer wore his.

Before the ambulance came into view, a police officer jogged around the corner and down the alley toward us.

"Step away from the body," he called, not noticing Amber had already completed his first task for him. As he arrived on the scene, he took one look at Clive's body and held a phone to his ear.

Help must have already been on its way because, by the time he hung up, two paramedics, three more police officers, and what I suspected was the medical examiner by his white lab coat headed our way. The alley was too narrow for driving, so the medical staff all carried cases of supplies with them.

One loudmouthed fiftysomething cop barked orders. "Get some crime scene tape up! Question the bystanders! And for the love of everything holy, don't let anyone touch anything!"

These cops seemed used to their boss and hurried to the business at hand.

"Those who were in the restaurant," one called, while another started wrapping yellow police tape around the area where the medical examiner loomed over Clive's body. "Please return to your seats and remain there until we have spoken to you!"

I was about to follow the crowd inside when the same officer called, "Mallory Beck?" and I froze in place, feeling like I was being accused of something. I nudged Amber toward the restaurant's door, even with my cat in tow. She obeyed without an argument.

I turned back and held up a hand. "That's me."

The officer took me by the arm and guided me away from the body and the people still gathered. Another officer called for those who had seen the man collapse to come forward.

No one did, and so he started at one end of the row of remaining bystanders with his notebook and pen poised. The officer with me wore a black suit, likely a detective. "I understand you called 911?"

"That's right," I told him.

"And can you please tell me how you came upon the incident and everything you saw?"

I took a breath and tried to pretend I was just telling everything to Alex back at home. "I was sitting inside when someone called from the door that Clive Richards, a man from our table, had collapsed in the alley."

"And this person at the door knew him by name?"

I had been attempting to keep Amber out of it, but it occurred to me that this tactic might only make her look guiltier.

"It was my traveling companion, a young teen named Amber Montrose.

She had been out taking my cat for a walk ..." I trailed off when the officer surveyed the crowd again, looking for Amber.

Hopefully, she'd had time to catch her breath. Then again, what would they expect from a sixteen-year-old who had stumbled across a dead body?

I pointed to the restaurant. "I told her to wait inside at our table."

He nodded and marched for the door. I followed, not about to let him question her alone. He continued to interview me on the way. "When you arrived outside, was anyone else out here?"

This was the part I didn't want to admit. But Alex had taught me that lies and half-truths would only hinder an investigation. "Not until people from the street and inside the restaurant made their way here."

He nodded, and I led him straight to Amber, who had Hunch on her lap and was nervously stroking him. Food and drinks had arrived at our table, but none of the six remaining tour participants touched them.

"Amber, this officer needs to ask about what you saw outside."

The officer scowled at me, not appreciating my warning. "Miss Montrose, can you please accompany me outside for a few questions?"

She stood, trying to hand Hunch over to me, but I suspected Hunch would keep her calm, so I said, "It's okay. I'm going with you."

Before the officer could argue this, I turned and told him, "She's sixteen, and I'm her guardian on this trip." Not legally, of course, but if he called her mother, it would take hours or even days for her to get onsite, and I was hopeful that

Helen Montrose wouldn't allow her daughter to be questioned alone.

The cop nodded and led us back outside. As Amber and I trailed behind, I murmured, "Where are your Mardi Gras beads?"

Her brow furrowed. "I was trying to play with Hunch and they broke."

I hoped they'd broken in our room or somewhere we could still find some proof that she hadn't used them to strangle Clive Richards.

The cop took us back to where he'd briefly questioned me. The outdoor crowd had thinned considerably in the last few minutes, so I could only assume they hadn't had much to tell.

I hoped this detective would understand quickly that he should look more closely at those currently seated at our table, and maybe even our waitress.

"I understand you knew the man you found collapsed in the alley?" the cop asked Amber.

"Mr. Richards was on a food tour with us. This was our third stop," Amber explained, stroking Hunch methodically.

The detective made a note. "So you just met Clive Richards today?"

Amber nodded, but my need to be helpful overshadowed my desire to stay in the background. "Actually, last night. We arrived at the hotel at nearly midnight, and the tour organizer introduced us to Clive Richards and his girlfriend, Scarlett, at that time."

The detective asked me for the name of our hotel and for the tour organizer's name. When he asked us to point out the girlfriend, Scarlett, and for her last name, we were unable to help.

"She left over an hour ago. She had to work at a local museum. I don't remember her last name, but I'm sure you can get it from Liam."

"Did anyone else from the tour seem to have prior knowledge of Mr. Richards?"

I started to shake my head, but then remembered. "Mr. Emile Dubois owns a restaurant in town, and Clive Richards had been a food critic in his restaurant. Monsieur Dubois didn't have any love for Clive Richards."

I hated throwing the sweet Frenchman under the bus, but then again, if he had truly followed Clive outside and strangled him, he wasn't a man I wanted to protect, no matter how nice he seemed.

"Mr. and Mrs. Kinsley didn't like him either," Amber told the detective. "He didn't have any patience for their diet restrictions."

"Clive even told them he believed in survival of the fittest, and those who couldn't handle regular food deserved to die off." I wasn't sure if those were the exact words.

The detective made a messily scrawled note and went on to question Amber about what she had seen when arriving back at the restaurant.

"Basically the exact same thing we're seeing now, but with less medics and police."

"Did you come close to the body or touch anything before you went into the restaurant and called your friend?"

She shook her head, but the detective squinted as though he didn't believe this.

Again, Helpful Mallory had to jump in to explain. "We've assisted with a few investigations in West Virginia. We both know better than to touch anything at a possible crime scene."

I wasn't sure the detective believed us, but he went on to ask about how long we planned to be in town and how we had ended up on the food tour.

"It was a prize in a recipe contest. Clive Richards was also a prize winner, I think, but you'd have to check with Liam O'Conner to confirm."

He asked about each of the other tour participants and their whereabouts when Mr. Richards left the table. Most of my answers were vague, except for with Amber, who I knew had gone to our hotel, and Lisa, who had been sitting at the table with me.

"And why had you brought your cat back to the restaurant?" the cop asked Amber.

That hadn't occurred to me, but it was a good question.

Amber looked down at Hunch as she answered. "He wanted to know where we were eating. He's a pretty curious cat, and he was pulling away from our hotel, so I said I'd show him."

Even though the words sounded completely believable to me, I knew before she'd finished explaining that Hunch wasn't your average cat, and the detective wouldn't put any stock in them.

"Gibson, you finished with everyone inside?" one of the other cops called.

The detective with us called over his shoulder. "Haven't even started. If you're finished out here, why don't you clear some of the people from the perimeter inside." It sounded like a directive, not a question.

Two other officers headed inside. The older ornery cop returned from his police car at the end of the alley and called out to the medical examiner as he walked toward him. "What do you say, Mitch? Can we move the body out of here yet?"

Gibson, the detective with us, asked about how long ago we had arrived at this restaurant, and I was glad the interruption had directed him away from our unbelievably strange cat. I spent a few seconds pretending to think about it because I wanted to hear Mitch-the-Medical-Examiner's answer.

Amber and I were the only nonofficial patrons in the alleyway, but Mitch-the-Medical-Examiner seemed to know how to keep the details of an investigation quieter than the brash fiftysomething cop.

The medical examiner murmured and held up a baggie with the green Mardi Gras beads inside, and the brash cop asked loudly, "What do you mean, that's not the cause of death?"

More quiet murmuring from the medical examiner and then, as he turned away, the gruff cop said, "Still, we gotta find out who had those green beads. Gibson?"

Detective Gibson cut his next question to us short. "Yes, sir?"

"Find out who had green Mardi Gras beads and who might be missing them."

We'd almost made it away from Detective Gibson without being asked about the beads. Now Amber would have to admit hers were green and they were missing.

I had a feeling Detective Gibson wasn't going to accept her excuse of playing with my cat.

Chapter Ten

DETECTIVE GIBSON LOOKED FIRST at me. "Is that the only strand of Mardi Gras beads you've had on your person today?"

I fingered the purple strand. "Yes, our waitress, Juliana, gave them to me. She had a bit of an altercation with Mr. Richards as well." I tried to deflect from Amber, but it didn't work.

"And you, Miss Montrose? Were you given Mardi Gras beads?"

"The waitress gave me a green strand, but when I went to get Hunch from the hotel room, he'd been lying around for the last hour, so I tried to get him playing out on the grass with the beads. Mallory's cat doesn't have much patience for playing, though. He swatted at them once, and they broke. I decided to take him for a walk and show him how close the restaurant we were eating at was instead."

"And which hotel was this?" Detective Gibson asked.

I told him the name and location.

"I'll have to ask you both to remain in the restaurant until one of our detectives can accompany you to your hotel."

We agreed and followed him inside. Of course, Amber's beads had to have been green and she had to have taken Hunch into the grass with them. I prayed that at least one of those beads would still be around and visible by the time we got there.

Or better yet, I prayed we'd find the true murderer and clear Amber's name.

The people from the perimeter of the restaurant were being quickly questioned and dismissed by the time we got inside. Amber and I were told to sit and wait at one of the outer tables, but that wouldn't give us much ability to hear the others being questioned.

I asked Detective Gibson, "Do you mind if I just grab our sandwiches?" I pointed at the two platters of cut-up po' boys.

He shrugged so I took that as a yes. Another detective was taking names and contact information from around our table. I took my time arranging all the po' boy portions onto one platter. Thankfully, the people at our table weren't as compliant as Amber and I had been and kept offering "helpful" information over the cop's basic questions.

"You should check with his girlfriend, Scarlett Marsh," Lisa told the cop. "If anyone wanted to strangle him, it was that girl."

The cop scribbled a note and turned back to Liam. "Mr. O'Conner, you were the leader of this food tour?"

Liam tried to answer, but Victoria Kinsley put in her two cents toward Lisa. "His girlfriend wasn't even here when it happened. You've been trash-talking Clive all day, so if they should look closer at anybody, maybe it should be you."

Detective Gibson, who had been listening in from nearby, stepped up to Lisa. "Ms. Lorenson? May I have a word with you over here, please?"

Lisa's eyes widened, first at Victoria, and then up at the police officer. "I—I was inside the whole time. Just ask Mallory!"

Lisa looked to me for confirmation, but as with all crime scenes, it seemed an automatic response to put my business hat on and emotionally distance myself from anyone involved. "I've already spoken to the detective," I told her. "Just tell him the truth."

Lisa took a deep breath and followed Detective Gibson across the restaurant to a table in the corner. I could no longer hear them, but by the way Lisa animatedly pointed back at Victoria, it wasn't hard to guess who she now suspected.

Victoria continued to speak to her husband about the awful situation, no longer throwing blame, but speaking loud enough that everyone at the table could hear. "I just think it's horrible that anyone would do that to anyone else." She didn't go so far as to use Clive's name or comment about his character, as that would have given a clear indication of her own motive.

Everyone ignored Emile Dubois, who sat quietly at the end of the table, reading something on his phone. No, he didn't look or act like a cold-blooded killer, but in my experience, that didn't always mean anything.

The brash older cop walked through the door. "Haven't you got this place cleared out yet?" He shook his head and strode for the kitchen area, where the restaurant staff huddled together whispering.

Juliana shook her head at the cop and motioned to her neck. When the cop questioned her further, all of the waitresses seemed to speak at once and all motioned to their necks.

I wished I were closer so I could hear whether they were talking about Clive being strangled with Mardi Gras beads, or if they were telling him the story of the pendant our waitress had asked him to remove.

A young cop strode for Liam. I continued taking my time with the food assembly to listen in, but a moment later, he led Liam to a table near where Amber sat. I had to decide quickly if it was more beneficial to stay and listen in on anything Victor, Victoria, and Monsieur Dubois had to say, which seemed the better plan, but for some reason, my instincts told me to follow our food tour leader. I hadn't spoken much to Liam on the tour, and I didn't know what kind of insight he had into the tour participants, but I followed my instincts, bringing one full platter of sandwiches back to Amber.

"Those look good," she said, but I held a finger to my lips. With my back turned to them, I motioned toward Liam and the cop as I slid into my chair.

In truth, our sandwiches looked a little past their prime already, which reminded me of my culinary arts teacher who called old food "mort." This reminded me of our waitress, but when I checked over my shoulder, the gruff police officer had already finished interviewing the wait staff.

I sighed back into my seat, straining to hear the conversation behind me. Amber glanced over my shoulder at regular intervals and leaned in, miming as though whispering to me, for the cop's benefit.

The cop asked Liam for a list of the full names of all the food tour participants and everything he knew about their relationship to Clive Richards. I sucked in a breath and held it when he started with my name.

"Mallory Beck and Clive Richards were winners in our magazine's recent original recipe contest. They were both awarded a tour for two people as well as a three-nights hotel stay."

But then Liam added something I didn't know. "Emile Dubois contested Mr. Richards' win, claiming the recipe came from his restaurant. He wanted our magazine to print a public correction, but our magazine editors feared litigation. Instead, we offered him a spot on the food tour."

"Was Emile Dubois still upset about this turn of events, in your opinion?" At least this cop was on the ball, going after Monsieur Dubois's motive. I wanted to turn around and tell him about the bad review Clive Richards had given of Monsieur Dubois's restaurant, but I kept myself rooted firmly in place, hoping to hear more.

"Not that I was aware." Liam's accent had become much less garish while talking with the police. "Victor and Victoria Kinsley signed up for the tour through our website. As far as I know, they'd not met Clive, but a quick tension developed there."

"What sparked the tension?"

Liam went on to explain Victoria Kinsley's food needs and Clive's annoyance. "To be fair, the lad was annoyed with lots of things: choice of restaurants, the Kinsleys' eating habits, and even young Amber's age."

I stiffened at the mention of Amber's name, but thankfully, the cop went on to ask, "Was there tension between you and Mr. Richards?"

A pause followed, and it was all I could do to keep from turning to see Liam's reaction. Liam had been exceedingly frustrated with Clive and perhaps even worried that Clive would get him fired.

"I wanted to see Mr. Richards satisfied, just like with any member of the tour," he finally said.

I looked forward to a time when I could add my own thoughts to the police's investigation. Not that I thought Liam O'Conner had killed Clive Richards. In fact, my impression from all the talk at our table was that Mr. Kinsley and Liam could vouch for each other's presence in the kitchen, and the chef would be able to confirm that. No one had spoken much about Victoria's whereabouts, which made me wonder if she was only pointing fingers at Lisa to deflect attention from where she had been during the murder.

There wasn't much else to learn from Liam. The cop seemed to realize this quickly, too, but before he could get his next interviewee into the chair behind me, Detective Gibson hovered at our table.

"We need to clear people out as soon as they've been questioned, so I'll walk you to your hotel now."

My heart dropped. I wanted to stay and figure this out. "Could I just, uh, pack these sandwiches up to go?"

"This is a police investigation, ma'am. I'm afraid we don't have time for that."

I bit my lip, feeling silly. Then again, the longer I stalled, the less chance of finding any stray green beads on the hotel's lawn.

"Okay, let's go." I stood and led the way to the door.

Chapter Eleven

CLIVE'S BODY HAD BEEN removed from the scene. Cell phone to his ear, the gruff cop paced back and forth along a small patch of the alleyway, talking loudly.

I stopped in place. "Oh! Just let me make sure I have my phone."

I checked through my purse as Amber let Hunch down on his leash. He immediately strained toward the crime scene tape.

"Slow-acting poison?" the gruff cop said into his phone. "If that's the case, couldn't it have been administered earlier today or even yesterday?"

Detective Gibson moved closer to his superior, and that gave Hunch a chance to get under the crime scene tape without notice. He sniffed around a small wet patch where Clive's face had been.

"Likely today?" The gruff cop relayed the information to Detective Gibson as he confirmed it into his phone. "You'll do a full autopsy and that'll reveal the timing, but you suspect within the last two hours?"

I bent down to elongate my purse search, but my head snapped up when the gruff cop said, "Hey! Get your cat away from there!"

My time was up. I stood, holding up my phone as though I'd just found it.

"I'm taking these ladies to their hotel to confirm the presence of some Mardi Gras beads," Detective Gibson told his superior.

His superior nodded. "Then question Mr. O'Conner about the earlier stops on the tour. I'll hold him until you get back."

Detective Gibson led us toward the busy street at the end of the alley. I quickly caught up beside him. "I think you should look more carefully at Emile Dubois. He was on the tour with us and owns his own local restaurant."

Detective Gibson gave me a side-eyed glance, which was all the encouragement I needed.

"Apparently, Clive Richards worked as a food critic and had given Monsieur Dubois's restaurant a scathing review. Plus, Clive Richards had stolen the recipe that had won him this food tour. He'd taken credit for it in a magazine. It's a pretty strong motive." I barely left a breath of space, for fear the detective wouldn't want to hear my theories. "Clive Richards was not an amiable guy. The Kinsleys also disliked him. And Clive had threatened to try and get Liam O'Conner fired earlier today."

Amber caught up, carrying Hunch. "At the Irish pub, Mr. Richards said he believed in survival of the fittest and basically if the Kinsleys couldn't eat a normal diet, they deserved to get sick and die. If that's not motive, I don't know what is."

"Monsieur Dubois was gone for a long time, claiming to be in the restroom," I added. "And our waitress, Juliana, had an argument with him, too."

Detective Gibson waved a hand. "Just over his pendant, which she claimed was cursed."

Cursed? That must've been the French word I didn't recognize. "Couldn't she have been involved in some way?"

"She'd been in the kitchen, trying to get one of the other waitresses to take her table. We questioned all the staff, but once folk like these get some voodoo theory in their head, it's hard to get them to talk about anything else."

I squinted at the weak excuse.

"The Kinsleys said they were with the chef," Amber said, "but I overheard Mr. Kinsley telling his wife to just say she was with him the whole time, which to me sounds like they planned to lie."

"When did you overhear this?" Detective Gibson asked.

"When I first got sent back into the restaurant. They were all talking about how it looked like Clive had been strangled to death." Amber turned to me. "It was when you were still talking to the police outside."

We arrived at our hotel parking lot, and Amber led the way across it to a small manicured green patch around the side that was lined with azaleas. She walked straight for where she must have been with Hunch. Only a second later, a few gleaming dots came into view. She pointed, but didn't pick any up. "See?"

The detective squatted near the beads, pulled out a plastic baggie, and scooped them up with a gloved hand.

I hoped this would put Amber in the clear as a suspect, but Detective Gibson's stern brow still made me nervous.

"Please wait at your hotel until you hear from us." He passed over a business card from the breast pocket of his suit jacket. "If you think of anything else of importance, give me a call. We're going to instruct Mr. O'Conner to cancel the rest of the food tour."

I forced a nod of agreement as my heart deflated. It made sense, but it still felt like such a loss. I hadn't even been allowed to pack up our po' boy sandwiches to eat at the hotel. Now the only New Orleans fare we'd get was whatever our hotel offered from room service.

"We'll be around if you need us," I told Detective Gibson. Amber hid Hunch under her sweater, and we headed around the corner to the hotel lobby as the detective strode purposefully away.

Chapter Twelve

ON THE WAY TO our room, Amber and I barely spoke, both disappointed about the canceled food tour. Once we had Hunch safely inside where he could emerge from under Amber's cardigan, she flopped back onto her bed and said, "I think we should call Alex."

I felt too scattered to put my thoughts about the day into any coherent order. I dropped onto my own bed and said, "Go for it."

She navigated to our detective friend's number within seconds. I lay back on my bed and listened as she explained the circumstances surrounding the probable murder.

"You two attract this sort of upheaval, don't you?" Alex asked through the speakerphone. It sounded lighthearted, as Alex could probably hear the exhaustion in Amber's tone, but the statement was too true for joking. We really were in the wrong place at the wrong time far too often.

Amber went on to describe the people involved, and I cataloged them all on the notepad from my purse as she did. Thorough notetaking might have been my only superpower, but it never failed to help me find points I had been missing.

Eventually, I chimed into the conversation, and Alex's voice brightened in response. "In my opinion, Emile Dubois is the prime suspect. He was alone, so he had opportunity, and he had more than one point of contention with Clive from long before the tour."

"Did he have means?" Alex asked. "Any access to poisons that you know of?"

I shook my head, even though Alex wouldn't be able to see it. "But how do we know any of them had access to a poison?"

"I'm not saying this Dubois character isn't your guy, but sometimes the most obvious suspect can be innocent."

I let that turn in my head. "He doesn't seem like a killer." I had said this plenty of times during prior investigations. Alex sighed quietly in response. He knew I'd argue myself enough on this point.

"What about that waitress who hated his pendant?" Amber asked. "She may have known where to find a poisonous cleaner around the restaurant."

"Plenty of cleaners are poisonous to ingest and could be slow-acting like the medical examiner suggested." Alex took a breath. "But it would be awfully hard to conceal in order to get a victim to ingest it. Do you want me to fly down there tomorrow? I have the day off. I'd just have to make sure Mickey can take Hunter."

Alex's incompetent partner wasn't much better with dog training than he was at detective work. "No, I'm sure the local police will tell us to go home by tomorrow." I sighed. "I'm not sure why we have to stay locked up in our hotel. I have a cell phone, so they can get a hold of us. I'd love one local meal before I go."

"I know if it was my investigation, I'd want to make sure all the other members of the group were safe."

I looked at Amber with a furrowed brow. "Why wouldn't we be safe?"

"No, no," he said. "I'm sure you are. They're probably just being cautious. If the killer thinks someone in the group heard or saw something, they might be tempted to threaten them." He didn't say the words "or worse," but I heard them.

His theory made sense.

After we'd talked the situation to death—no pun intended—Alex told us to stay together and be safe before he hung up. I looked at my long list of notes and felt a little more clearheaded, but still couldn't pinpoint the killer.

"We need food," Amber said. "Brain energy."

She was right. The food from our first two stops had long ago digested. I generally couldn't eat much when working on a case, but I had to keep Amber fed.

Just then a knock sounded at our door.

I looked at Amber, but then popped up off my bed. I wasn't about to let her answer it.

Liam stood on the other side. Worry lines creased his forehead. "Ah, Mallory." His voice was that overly musical version of itself again. "I'm glad I found ya. The police have arranged for a hospitality room for the rest of us to spend some time while they investigate. The hotel restaurant has sent over gobs of food. I thought you and Amber might be hungry."

Although I didn't seriously suspect Liam of murder, I remembered what both Detective Gibson and Alex said about not going places alone. "The others are there?"

"Just Lisa, so far, but the rest will arrive when they're done being questioned."

I nibbled my lip. I didn't like the idea of leaving Lisa there on her own. "Sure," I finally said. "Let me just grab my purse."

Liam hadn't been kidding about the gobs of food. Two end-to-end tables were heaped with it along an entire wall. Unfortunately, from one glance, I could tell that the hamburgers and spaghetti type of features weren't going to stretch my palette. On the way, I had worried about a slow-acting poison in the food, but two waitresses were there to assist with the serving.

In the time that Liam had come to retrieve us, the Kinsleys had also made their way back to the hospitality suite. They hovered over the food display, discussing every item with seriousness.

"Why don't you grab something?" I murmured to Amber. "Listen in for anything important. Meanwhile, I'll have a word with Lisa."

Amber headed for the food display, and I moved toward where Lisa sat alone on a sofa. I wondered if she'd already eaten or if she was too distraught to eat. Liam headed back out to watch for Monsieur Dubois, but with everyone else here, I had to believe the police may have arrested him by now.

"Did you get some food?" I sat across from Lisa on the couch.

She shook her head. "I can't eat. Not with everything that's happened." Even though I related to her on that point, part of me still wondered if it could indicate some guilt. But before I could open my mouth to ask anything else, she gave me her best theory. "You know what I think?" She barely allowed time for my shrug. "I think Scarlett didn't even have to work today. I think she left because she was sick of the way Clive treated her."

Clive's girlfriend had been completely off my radar, as she hadn't even been in the vicinity when he collapsed.

"I'll bet he went outside to call her and tell her to get her butt back to the restaurant. She didn't even mention having to work until we were outside and ready to move to the next stop. She wasn't giving him a chance to argue."

Amber had taken a seat at a round table across from the Kinsleys with very different-looking plates of food. Amber's was heaped with a hamburger and fries, while the Kinsleys' looked to be almost all vegetables. I was willing to bet Amber would nail down the truth about the Kinsleys' alibis by the time she finished her plate.

I eyed Lisa. A bit talkative for investigative work, but her suspicious nature could work in her favor. "So you think if we went to Scarlett's job, she wouldn't actually be there?" It wasn't a completely far-fetched idea. "But Scarlett didn't tell you she lied about having to work, right?"

Lisa didn't have a chance to answer, as the door opened right then. Emile Dubois stood in the doorway.

Why was he back here so quickly? Why hadn't they arrested him or at least held him for further questioning? Had Detective Gibson ignored everything we'd told him?

Monsieur Dubois headed for the food, and so I stood to meet him there, my conversation with Lisa all but forgotten. "Did the police instruct you to leave the restaurant?"

"Oui, and to come straight back here to the hotel." He took a step back toward the door, as if wanting to get away from me.

"Just a few questions first." I stepped around him, blocking his path to the door. "Did Clive Richards win the food tour by submitting your recipe?"

Monsieur Dubois sighed. "It is true, but there is no way to prove such a thing. Especially not now."

"But you must have been angry when you saw it in Foodie Elite Magazine. Did you come on the tour to confront the man who stole from you?"

His gaze dropped to the carpet, perhaps processing his strong motive for murder. But Alex's reminder came back to me: It's often not the most obvious suspect.

I tried a new angle. "And where were you when he died?" Even if he were poisoned earlier in the day, someone had to have doubled those Mardi Gras beads around his neck so tightly they'd left impressions.

"There was a problem at my restaurant. I was on my cellular phone in the lobby discussing it."

I raised an eyebrow in disbelief. "What was the problem?" A non-kitchen-savvy police officer might not know to ask this.

"My sous-chef had an accident and had to go to l'hôpital. He was impossible to replace on short notice."

"Why the hospital?" I assumed a knife cut, but quickly reminded myself not to lead the questioning, as Alex had taught me. "Was it serious?"

He shrugged in a very French, very vague way. "Mais oui. Eric slipped on some water that had boiled over. He caught another pot with his fall and toppled it onto himself. He has some third-degree burns."

Without meaning to, one of my hands flew to my mouth. When I worked at Antonia's Restaurant, one of our line cooks had been badly burned and rushed to the hospital. I blinked and reminded myself of my purpose. "Who did you talk to at the restaurant when you called?"

"I spoke with my chef, Martin. My maître d' had already taken Eric to the hospital, and they were très short on staff. I called in a junior chef, and I gave my staff les instructions to give complimentary entrée or dessert to anyone who had attend longtemps—that is, waited a long time."

The explanation was thorough enough that it could be true. Maybe I should spend a moment trying to prove Monsieur Dubois's innocence, rather than his guilt.

"Are the police going to check with your chef about this phone call?"

"Perhaps." He sounded much less concerned than I thought he should be.

"Did anyone see you on your phone before Amber came in calling about the incident?"

"Ah, yes. Madame Kinsley."

"Victoria? What was she doing there?"

"She did not seem to notice my serious phone conversation. She studied the restaurant's menu in the lobby and kept telling me how ridiculous that she had come to a restaurant specializing in sandwiches."

I raised an eyebrow. "Victoria was in the lobby the whole time."

"As much as I noticed, oui. And she did not seem to want to stop letting me notice."

Any other time, I might have found this picture entertaining, but for the moment, I only felt relief.

Perhaps Emile Dubois wasn't guilty of murder.

But if not Monsieur Dubois or Victoria Kinsley, then who?

Chapter Thirteen

AMBER AND I SPENT another half hour in the hospitality room interviewing all the people from our food tour, as well as Liam when he returned from making some phone calls to his food tour company.

Finally, we both claimed tiredness and said we were going to rest in our room. What we really planned to do was compare notes.

"It has to be either Mr. Dubois or Mrs. Kinsley who killed Clive Richards," Amber murmured as soon as we were alone in the hallway together.

I dug out my key card. "That's what I thought, too, but I had an interesting conversation with Emile Dubois. It turns out Monsieur Dubois and Victoria had both been in the entryway of the restaurant before you discovered Clive's body."

"They must have been in it together!"

Hunch sat at attention just inside our hotel room. I hated bursting Amber's bubble, but we had to get to the truth. "I don't think so. Monsieur Dubois was on the phone with his restaurant the whole time. The police would be able to confirm that. He said Victoria kept interrupting him. It didn't sound like they were on the same team."

I pulled out my notepad. As I worked out the alibis, I spoke them aloud. "If Monsieur Dubois and Victoria could vouch for each other's presence, and Victor and Liam O'Conner were with the chef...Plus, I was having a conversation at the table with Lisa... That leaves..." I scanned through my list of suspects, but Amber filled in the blank.

"That leaves me, Mallory." She crossed her arms. "The only person who doesn't have an alibi is me."

Chapter Fourteen

MY GAZE RACED OVER the notepaper because that simply couldn't be the case. Besides, Detective Gibson had found Amber's green Mardi Gras beads.

"The waitress, Juliana!" I suddenly blurted. "Or Scarlett Marsh." I dug into my purse for the discount card she had given us.

"She had gone to work by the time Mr. Richards collapsed," Amber reminded me. "You're reaching, Mallory. And it sounded like that waitress was scared to go anywhere near Mr. Richards and his cursed pendant. Why would she have chased him outside?"

Something Lisa had said came back to me. "Scarlett claimed to have gone to work. And Clive could have been poisoned earlier in the day. One of these museums is a pharmacy museum." I looked over the list of six museums. "If she worked at that one, she may have had access to poisons."

Amber was still unconvinced. "Scarlett hadn't been given any Mardi Gras beads, green or not."

"The beads don't seem all that difficult to find. All the waiters and waitresses had access to them. They were even draped on that statue on our way to the restaurant." I stood from where I'd been perched on the edge of my bed. "The statue!"

Amber looked at me with her brow furrowed.

This was definitely reaching, but I said it anyway. "What color of Mardi Gras beads were on the trombone-player statue near the alley? Do you remember?"

Amber shrugged and pulled out her phone. "Beats me. But I think I took a picture."

I hurried over. Sure enough, she'd snapped a photo of the busy street, including the statue. Zooming in, we could see the statue had three strands of beads: one gold, one purple, and one green.

"You took this on our way to the restaurant? You wouldn't have taken this while you were walking Hunch?"

She balked. "That cat has a mind of his own when he's on the leash. Believe me, I wasn't taking pictures."

"I think I should go check that statue."

We weren't supposed to leave the hotel, and if the police spotted either of us near the scene of the crime, that could shed a lot more suspicion on us. But if we didn't do our own investigating, what were the chances the detectives wouldn't soon return to suspecting Amber?

I had to find a way to prove her innocence before the trail led back to her.

Chapter Fifteen

"I CAN'T JUST STAY here while you go out there and get yourself killed or arrested!"

Leave it to a teenager to be so dramatic. "Nobody's getting killed or arrested. In fact, I thought I might be able to get a clear enough view of the statue if I took my car, and then I won't be so obvious if the police are still around. After that, I can go by that pharmacy museum and see if Scarlett works there and if anyone could confirm her presence all afternoon."

Amber flopped onto her bed. "But I want to go, too!"

I didn't blame her, but I also didn't want to let on about my worry over her being a serious suspect. "Someone has to be here to answer the phone in case the police call, and you can't drive on your own."

"I could walk and stay out of sight." I opened my mouth to rebut, but no words came. Then she interrupted my thoughts with, "But I suppose you're right. Since you have an alibi and I don't, I probably shouldn't be the one snooping around the crime scene."

Why I'd thought my concerns would get past my teenage sleuthing brainiac friend, I'd never know.

I left her with an instruction not to answer the door for anybody. Even if someone claimed to be a police officer, she would say I was in the shower and tell them we'd meet them in the lobby in a few minutes. Then she'd text me and tell me to get my butt back here.

Ten minutes later, I drove toward the Café N.O. Amber had insisted I bring Hunch, I suspected to protect me. In truth, it wouldn't be the first time if he did.

He sat on his haunches in the passenger seat, barely reacting to the movement, no matter how sharply I took the corners.

As the sun was setting, the French Quarter had filled significantly with partygoers. It was all I could do to avoid hitting any pedestrians who stumbled in front of my car. It took much longer than it would have taken walking. With tight one-way streets, it took me forever to wind my way back to the statue. In fact, I only realized I'd found it when Hunch growled.

In a quick glimpse, and with dusk falling, it was impossible to tell what color beads adorned the statue.

Parking in the French Quarter had also filled in the last couple of hours. I finally found a parking garage with some space on the top floor.

I had Hunch's leash in my purse, but I told him as I scooped him up into my arms, "If you don't fuss, I'll keep you off the leash."

He raised his eye whiskers at me, and I could imagine him replying, "If you're a good girl, Mallory, I'll let you tag along on my investigation."

With the flood of people, it took several minutes to return to the alleyway, but at least Hunch and I would no longer be as obvious snooping around.

We came at the statue from across the street, and I squinted at the strands of beads. I could make out purple and gold, but had to get closer to see if the green ones were still there.

By the time I got close to the statue, people nudged and pushed me on every side, but I stood my ground as my cat sniffed toward the two strands of beads looping the statue.

The green one was missing.

I snapped a quick photo before poking my head around the statue and down the alley. Groupings of people stood smoking and blocked my view of the crime scene. I couldn't even tell if the restaurant had opened again.

Hunch wrestled in my arms, trying to get back to that crime scene tape.

"I can't go down there," I murmured to him.

He growled in response and dug his claws into my arm.

I jerked and let him go. My dress was sleeveless, and my arm already showed beads of blood. It wasn't the first time Hunch had clawed me, but as he crept along the side of the alley toward the crime scene tape, I reminded myself that he only ever did it with an investigative purpose.

Once Hunch disappeared from view, I felt too nervous to stay so far away from him. I edged my way around the statue, keeping a keen eye out for any of the cops who might recognize me.

I stayed close to the brick wall, but I didn't see Hunch anywhere.

Something rubbed against my bare leg, and relief washed over me. I looked down and even bent to pick him up before I realized it was a bony brown cat, probably a stray.

The cat had ignored everyone else in the alley and headed straight for me. Great. I really was becoming a cat lady.

"Shoo!" I whispered to him. "Go find my cat!"

He sniffed the air a couple of times, then started off deeper into the alley.

I wondered if I'd inadvertently started a cat fight. Now I had to get closer—not that I was eager to get in the middle of all those claws. I spotted Hunch coming back toward me with something in his mouth. No sooner had I let out my breath than I glanced back toward the statue and saw Amber waving, trying to get my attention.

What on earth? She knew better than to show up here when she was already a suspect. Unless...she had come up with some new information.

Just as I scooped Hunch up, Amber's gaze darted past me down the alley.

Detective Gibson hadn't noticed me yet, but he was marching straight for Amber!

I picked up in a run toward Amber. She rounded the statue out of sight. As soon as I got to the statue, partygoers blocked my view, but I kept moving, searching every direction for her.

Half a block along, an arm reached out and grabbed me, yanking me into a tiny shop. I yelped, but then saw it was Amber.

"You can't be here!" I hissed. We moved away from the open door of the souvenir shop filled with voodoo trinkets. "Why did you leave our room?"

"Detective Gibson called! He said he'd be by in forty-five minutes. You didn't reply to my text and I had to get to you before then!"

The cacophony around me must have drowned out my text notification. Not only would we not be peacefully waiting for Detective Gibson in our room, but he now knew we were sneaking around the crime scene.

This didn't look good for us at all.

"We were right about the beads on the statue," I told her. "The green one was missing. It could have been anyone from the street who strangled Clive."

"Or it could have been me." She raised an eyebrow. "What about the pharmacy museum? Did you find Scarlett? She could have grabbed some beads from the statue. She would have come from the street, and she had more motive than any of us to kill Mr. Richards."

Why hadn't I searched out the museums first? I had been convinced the statue would lead us to the truth.

But it was too late to investigate our theories because Detective Gibson stood in the doorway of the souvenir shop, looking straight at us.

Chapter Sixteen

"YOU LADIES ARE COMING with me." Detective Gibson grabbed each of us by the arm.

"Just give me a chance to explain," I told him.

"You can tell me all about it down at the station." He pushed us out the door and down the street toward his unmarked police car.

I tried to avoid oncoming foot traffic, but the toe of my ballet flat caught on an uneven patch of sidewalk, and I careened forward. I caught myself before hitting the asphalt, but in the process, Hunch dug his claws into my arm again.

Despite the pain, I held tight. Out in this crowd, I'd have no chance of finding him after Detective Gibson drove us to the police station.

"Please don't," I gritted out to my cat instead. But when I glanced down at him, he stretched his mouth wide like he did when trying to throw up a hairball.

Right! Hunch had something in his mouth, something he'd found around the crime scene!

"Spit it up, Hunch," I instructed.

We reached Detective Gibson's car, and he looked between me and my cat before sighing and pulling a rear door open. "I don't suppose you could contain your cat's regurgitations to the floor mat?"

"I'll try," I told him, even though I had no objection to Hunch puking any place he felt like, especially if it produced a clue to this murder.

Once we were in the backseat, I murmured to Amber, "Hunch has something in his—"

My words were cut off by Detective Gibson. "I'll ask you to please keep quiet until we reach the station."

It took nearly twenty minutes to drive less than a couple of miles to the nearest precinct. As much as I didn't want to drag Alex into this, I considered asking Detective Gibson to call him, just so we'd get the opportunity to explain our infraction.

By the time we got out of the police car, Hunch looked less like he needed to cough anything up. I envisioned myself in a prison cell a week from now, picking through Hunch's excrement with a twig, looking for the clue that could have saved us.

We followed Detective Gibson the short walk from the parking lot to the four-story police headquarters. Even though night had fallen, lit windows showed a busy office that was much more intimidating than the small Honeysuckle Grove one.

He led us to a small interrogation room, very much like I'd seen on TV— nothing but an empty table, four chairs, and a glass window we couldn't see through.

"Listen," I said before we'd sat down. "I know this looks bad, but we have a good explanation."

"You have an explanation of why you were downtown when I specifically instructed you to stay in your hotel?" Before I could answer, he went on. "You have an explanation of where your young friend was at the time of the murder of Clive Richards? Because we have more than one witness claiming he had publicly humiliated her less than an hour before he was found dead."

Detective Gibson kept his eyes on me as he spoke, not glancing at Amber once. He was likely treading carefully, knowing the delay it would cause if I claimed Amber's mother should be here.

I'd play that card, too, but only if I had to.

I passed Hunch to Amber, needing to give this conversation my full focus. Hunch, the traitor, immediately purred in her arms.

"Listen, Detective, I know you're just doing your job, and I know this because we regularly help our local police department back home." Here goes nothing. Time to drag Alex into this.

But a choking sound interrupted my next words. I turned as Hunch worked at bringing something up again. Amber squatted to the floor to let him down.

"Please sit, and I'll do the talking from now on." Detective Gibson wore a look of distaste as he watched Hunch. He'd have to clean up whatever came out of his suspect's cat.

"We will," I said, but then I squatted near Hunch, too. "I...just...I think my cat is about to choke up an important clue."

The sigh Detective Gibson let out didn't convey confidence. But Hunch had proven to us he had a nose for investigative work. Returning to me so quickly from the crime scene could only mean he'd found something important.

While Hunch coughed and Amber cooed over him, I offered the best explanation I could. "I know it's hard to believe, but my cat really can sniff out clues as good as any police dog I've ever met." Granted, I'd only ever met one police dog, but Detective Gibson didn't know that. "Clive Richards made snide comments to everyone on the tour— including our tour guide. Everyone disliked the man, but in only knowing him one day, who actually had a motive to kill him? And who had access to a poison? Certainly not my sixteen-year-old friend."

I didn't leave time for him to respond. "Emile Dubois had a substantial grudge against the man that started well before the food tour. He's local and knows food, and perhaps could have concealed a poison. Victoria Kinsley suffered from depression and how upsetting do you think it had been when Clive mocked her food intolerances? He had even threatened the leader of the food tour about getting him fired. Did you question Liam O'Conner about that?"

It surprised me when the detective nodded. "Mr. O'Conner told us about the threat. He also told us that his company, Foodie Elite, was the one taking bribes from restaurants in order to place them on the tour, so he had no fear of getting fired. Besides, all those people you've mentioned have alibis. Your friend here doesn't."

I didn't let his words deter me. "Mr. Richards also humiliated his girlfriend many times."

"Scarlett Marsh?" Detective Gibson looked over his notepad.

I was so surprised he was listening to me, I stood and rooted through my purse until I found the discount museum card.

He ignored the card and held out a hand. "I'd like to search both of your purses, please."

I slid mine across the table and then reached for Amber's. We had nothing to hide.

He searched them quickly, as though looking for something specific, and then passed them back.

I slid the discount card another inch toward him. "Scarlett works at a local museum. My next stop was going to be to see if she did go to work and if she happened to work at the pharmacy museum, only a short walk from Café N.O."

Detective Gibson studied the card. "You were at the crime scene trying to perform your own investigation."

I couldn't tell if it was a question. "It's what we do back in West Virginia."

"Well, I don't know how they handle police work in West Virginia, but in Louisiana, we let the trained detectives handle our investigations." He twisted his lips, still staring at the card.

"But we found something," Amber said. "Don't forget the statue."

Detective Gibson looked at me. "The statue?"

I explained the missing strand of beads and showed him the before and after photos, with and without the green beads. "If you still have an officer on site, have him go and look. Maybe take some fingerprints."

Detective Gibson held his phone to his ear. Not only did he tell the person on the line to check the statue, but he also asked him to go by the pharmacy museum and find out if a Scarlett Marsh had been working today.

Scarlett Marsh still felt like a long shot, but she was all we had.

At least until a moment later, when Hunch let out one loud hack and chucked up an antique button with a leaping dog in the center.

Chapter Seventeen

THE POLICE DIDN'T CATCH up with Scarlett Marsh at her job at the New Orleans historical pharmacy museum, where she hadn't been scheduled to work on this particular Saturday. Instead, they caught up with her at her apartment, not far from downtown.

She'd been calming her shaken nerves with a bottle of wine, and it hadn't been difficult for Detective Gibson to talk a confession out of her about finally getting rid of the boyfriend who had belittled and threatened her for months.

When Clive went outside the restaurant and called her cell phone, she had been lurking nearby. He saw her and came after her. She grabbed for the Mardi Gras beads from the statue to fend him off. If not for the poison in his system, he would have been too strong for her.

Detective Gibson also found three empty bottles of eye drops in her purse that she hadn't bothered to discard.

We heard the details late the next day when Detective Gibson visited us in our hotel restaurant to let us know we were free to stay in town or travel home. Unfortunately, with an upcoming catering job in West Virginia, we had to leave. Alex had told me detectives weren't supposed to share detailed information, but now that Detective

Gibson was doing it as well, I had to wonder if Amber and I somehow emanated trustworthiness.

"So she really poisoned him with Visine?" Amber asked. We'd left Hunch in our hotel room, but he'd get to hear all the details on our long drive home.

"Our medical examiner suspected tetrahydrozoline, a substance found in many over-the-counter eye drops. He won't be able to confirm it until the lab reports return."

"That's why you searched our purses?" I asked.

He nodded. "The medical examiner had never seen a fatal case of tetrahydrozoline poisoning. Miss Marsh claimed she only wanted to make him sick, but as an employee at a pharmacy museum, we suspect she would have known the large amount she gave him would have been deadly. It's a difficult taste to mask, so we still haven't worked out how she got him to take it yet."

"The pepper eating contest!" Amber said.

I went on to explain how several gentlemen, including Clive, had taken part in a hot pepper eating contest at the Irish pub. "She must have put the poison in his drink while he was trying to buy one of the prize T-shirts."

Detective Gibson looked as satisfied as Alex usually did when his investigations clicked into place. "I wouldn't wish for you to be involved in another murder investigation in our city, but we're appreciative of your help. If you wanted to seriously pursue a future in investigative work..." With this statement, he looked at Amber. "You'd do well with it. We'd even welcome the help of your cat."

"Yeah, this wasn't our first rodeo." Amber easily took the praise.

After Detective Gibson left, Amber and I packed up. We had to get home in time to do a big shop for our catering event.

"Home sounds good about now, doesn't it?" I asked Amber.

She tucked Hunch into her duffel bag and headed for the hotel room door. "Yeah, but maybe we could come back again and actually try some local food sometime when murder isn't on the menu?"

I laughed. "Sounds good. But it is a long drive back to Honeysuckle Grove. What do you say we find somewhere that serves a po' boy to go?"

The End

Witchy Wednesday (Preview)

IF YOU ENJOYED MALLORY Beck's cozy adventures, you'll love Tabitha Chase and the witchy cast of the Days of the Week Mysteries. Order Witchy Wednesday, the first in this new series now or turn the page to read an excerpt!

**Witchy Wednesday
A Tabitha Chase Days of the Week
Mystery (Book 1)**

The murder of a witch, a seaside town selling the supernatural, and a realtor-turned-sleuth rediscovering her purpose...

When self-proclaimed realist and realtor Tabitha Chase takes a trip to small-town Crystal Cove to sell her late aunt's houseboat, nothing is what it seems on the surface, including a local witch's cause of death.

Tabby's spreadsheets and staging skills won't solve the case, but her newly inherited psychic cat might. With the help of a fetching forensics expert and a dashing detective, Tabby hopes to clear her name from suspicion and discover the truth.

Join this witchy cast of characters in the small beach town of Crystal Cove where Tabby may be the only person who can see past the shroud of illusions.

Chapter One

When I was a little girl, my Auntie Lizzie told me there were two ways to get to Crystal Cove, Oregon—over the mountains on the Interstate or the way she arrived: on a broomstick across the skies. As an eight-year-old, I'd wanted to believe her stories with everything in me despite the forewarnings of my pragmatic parents. Through the years, and many real-world obstacles, I'd come to the understanding those stories were only the fodder of elaborate make believe, by people who chose to focus on the imaginary instead of looking head-on at their real life problems. My learning had become complete a month ago when Aunt Lizzie left a note for her sister, my mom, and then jumped off of Crystal Falls to her death.

Crystal Cove used to hold an awe and mystique like Disneyland, but as I descended the 101 out of the Calapooya Mountains through rain so slick I could barely see the front of my car, to take care of some post mortem details, I decided the last tiny part of me that believed in magic had officially died with my aunt.

My windshield wipers squeaked at regular intervals and my old Honda smelled awful with exhaust, having worked harder than she had in a long time to get up and through the mountain passes. My hands were white-knuckle locked on my steering wheel and I'd been squinting at the road in front of me for almost three hours. This road demanded a lot more than autopilot, but I jumped in my seat when my phone rang through the Bluetooth, letting me know I'd better clue back in.

I fumbled over my phone, not looking away from the road for even a second, and answered, "Hi, Dad. I'm almost there."

The pause that followed made me glance down at my phone screen for one quick heartbeat. Shoot. I'd done it again. It wasn't my dad, who knew all about my trip to Crystal Cove, and had pretty much forced it upon me. Nope. It was my boss, Brendan Reiger, who had yet to hear about my impromptu trip and who I had planned to explain it to much more delicately as soon as I had the chance.

"Almost...where, Tabitha?" Brendan said through my car's speakers. He had a deep, almost ominous voice. All the realtors in our Portland office thought it was the authority that came with that kind of voice that helped him make so many quick sales. His voice sounded even deeper tonight, which made me momentarily forget my strategic wording and blurt out the truth.

"Oh, yes, well, I just had to take a quick trip down the coast. I, um. I had a death in the family." I hoped he wouldn't ask how recent the death was. I suspected if I had to explain that Aunt Lizzie died over a month ago, he'd lack the bit of sympathy I had hoped to garner from my tough-as-nails boss.

Instead, he said, "Oh. Who died?"

I blinked hard, trying to split my attention between the rain-soaked road and this phone call. I really should have pulled over—if only I could see the shoulder. "It was my Aunt Lizzie." My voice came out more full of drama than I intended, which only made Brendan pry more.

"Right. Were you close, then?"

I couldn't, in good conscience, say yes. I hadn't seen my aunt in years. But instead I searched for something that might seem like the affirmative. "She was my mom's little sister." Again with the drama, Tabby? Take some acting lessons already!

"And you'll be back tomorrow? We have that showing in Stafford and I hoped I could count on you for putting up signage."

Putting up signage. Was that what my job had become? I'd been giving the Portland real estate market all I had for the last three years. I spent late nights and early mornings drafting market reports and perfecting my staging skills. At every turn, Brendan suggested I'd be his next superstar realtor, but then he'd saddle me with staging rundown townhouses, blowing up balloons for open houses, and now putting up signage.

"Um, it's a long drive," I said, as I passed a weathered wooden sign with faded paint boasting: WELCOME TO CRYSTAL COVE. The road was shrouded with trees on either side and my GPS showed a few miles yet before I'd reach the town center and then the marina. There were no streetlights out this far and I continued to squint to see through the rain as I berated myself for picking up the call. "So I probably won't make it back by tomorrow."

"By Tuesday then." It didn't sound like a question. When I didn't say anything right away, he went on. "Our office has been talking to a client from Forest Park. I think they're ready to list, and wouldn't that be the perfect neighborhood for your first solo listing? Wouldn't that make your dad proud?"

My heart rate sped up, both from the idea of my own listing, in Forest Park no less, and from the idea of my father being proud. He was a state senator and with his endless connections, he'd offered to get me a job with a local realtor as soon as I'd passed the exam, but I'd refused, wanting to prove myself and make my own way in the real estate world. More than once, I'd regretted that quick decision, but now I let a breath seep out of me slowly. Maybe it was time to finally see some fruits from my labor.

I'd barely let out my breath when an obstruction in the middle of the road made me slam on my brakes. I shrieked as the form of a woman came into view. She was lying right in the middle of the rain-soaked road.

"Tabitha?" Brendan asked. "I can count on you to be back on Tuesday, right?"

"I—uh—I have to go." I couldn't tune into Brendan's reply as I slammed my car into Park, grabbed for my phone, and got out of my car. I left it running, with the windshield wipers working furiously trying to keep up with the rain and the headlights aimed toward the woman. As I moved closer and pulled the hood of my jacket up over my head, she appeared dead—face up, but with one of her jean-clad legs out at an odd angle—spread almost to the splits and bent upward at the knee, clearly broken. The odd angles of this woman's body in the midst of the brutal storm with the narrow lighting of my headlights made me momentarily see the situation as a meticulously planned movie. I blinked and then shook my head at myself, reminding myself this was real.

"Hello? Hello? Are you okay?" I called. My heart rate ratcheted up as I moved closer and looked into her unblinking eyes, being splattered with raindrops. She had striking features—red full lips and thick eyelashes. She looked so alive. My phone was still in my hand, getting soaked, so I tucked it under my jacket and dialed 911. A second later, a woman answered.

"911. What is your emergency?"

"There's a woman. In the middle of the road. I don't think she's breathing."

The operator asked me for my location and I tried to think as I bent to get closer to the woman. She wore a bright yellow poncho that looked hand knit. It immediately made me wonder who knit it for her—who would be devastated by the news of her passing.

"Um. Off highway 101. Just past the Welcome sign to Crystal Cove."

I reached for the woman's wrist as the operator confirmed my location. Fresh out of college, I'd attempted a short career as a personal trainer. I'd taken a fitness first aid course, at that point, but it felt like a million years ago. Still, training or no training, I knew not finding a pulse was bad news. I explained this to the operator. She instructed me to wait where I was and an emergency vehicle would arrive as soon as possible. After hanging up, I reached for the woman's neck. She was still warm, but I couldn't find a pulse there either. When I pulled my hand away, it was covered in rain mixed with blood.

The metallic scent hit my nose and I gagged. I'd never been great with the sight or smell of blood, and in an instant, I was up and backed up against the hood of my car, trying to keep my dinner from three hours ago down in my stomach where it belonged. I kept my eyes from my bloodied hand for long enough that I could catch my breath, and hoped the rain would wash the bulk of the blood off before I had to look at it, but the sky chose this moment to close up and stop its torrential downpour.

"Great, the one time I actually want the rain," I murmured toward the sky. My windshield wipers squeaked against the drying glass as I moved back toward my driver's door and found a napkin in the door storage with my left hand while holding my right hand as far as possible away from my nose. I flicked off the wipers, then I held my breath as I wiped off the blood and looked around for somewhere I could dispose of the dirtied napkin.

Never usually one to litter, tonight I couldn't help myself. I tossed it into the roadside bushes, as the metallic smell was still playing awful tricks on my stomach. I bent to douse my hand in a nearby puddle as sirens sounded in the distance. My headlights caught something blue and gleaming right beside the puddle.

I picked up the tiny jewel and studied it. It probably wasn't worth anything, but it seemed like glass, maybe that sea glass my aunt used to tell me about, and so I tucked it into my jacket pocket and stood as the sirens grew louder and I tried to collect myself.

I walked a wide circle around the woman on the ground, taking note of any details that might be helpful for the ambulance upon its arrival. On her front side, the woman appeared soaked from the rain, but otherwise unmarked. Her hair was a strawberry blonde, less red than mine, but still red enough to make out the hue even while soaking wet and lit only by my headlights. Now that the rain had subsided, the blood on her neck was visible. Her eyes remained eerily open, now looking up at the sky as though she might be waiting to be taken up to heaven.

A firetruck arrived on scene first. It parked at an angle and two burly firemen emerged from the front doors. A third fireman came around from the back of the truck headed straight for me.

"Are you alright? What happened here? Are you injured?"

"No, I'm fine. I didn't hit the woman. She was like this when I arrived." I'd been leaning over to see if I could find anything else of this woman's injuries, but as the fireman moved between me and the woman, I didn't hesitate to take several large steps back.

One of the other firemen quickly set up a large pot light on a stand, lighting up several feet in all directions of the woman.

"And your name?" the first fireman asked me. He had a square jaw and was clean-shaven, unlike his two coworkers.

"Tabitha..." I hesitated, as my father had drilled into me about a thousand times to keep the Chase name as quiet as possible on this trip. But the fireman kept staring at me, a pen poised over his notepad, so I had no choice but to add, "Chase. Tabitha Chase."

Before the fireman could ask me anything more, a dark sedan with blue and red flashing lights and siren screaming whipped around the corner and parked sideways, blocking the road behind my car. The firetruck was at an angle, blocking most of the road in the other direction, which left all five of us, plus the woman's body, in a small cocoon of space.

A man in a suit, I guessed him to be a detective, emerged from the dark sedan, came around my car, and set his dark eyes squarely on the unshaven fireman. "Tell me what we've got here, Tucker," he said, and it sounded more like an order than a question.

"Just arrived on scene, sir."

"Looks like posterior injuries," one of the bearded firemen called out from where he was bent near the woman.

"She's bleeding on the back of her neck," I volunteered helpfully.

The detective's head snapped toward me. "Did you move the body?"

I shook my head. "No, of course not. I just checked for a pulse."

The detective's brow furrowed, like he wasn't sure he believed me. He also reached to check for a pulse, but on her wrist. "Is this the exact placement the woman fell to?" He stood again and loomed over me.

"I—I guess so."

His eyes drilled into me, waiting for more. "Did you move her legs?"

"No! I mean, I just found her like this."

Again with the furrowed brow. "You didn't hit her with your vehicle?"

"No, she was already here," I said again.

"No pulse. Posterior trauma," the clean-shaven fireman said, still making notes. "Mick should be here soon."

The detective nodded and yelled at one of the bearded firemen, who was tilting up the woman's body to have a look at her back. "Are you kidding me, Johnson? Don't move her!" He turned back to the clean-shaven fireman—Tucker—who seemed to be in charge of the firetruck contingent. "She was struck down?" He flipped open his own notebook and started writing before Tucker had started to answer.

"Well, no, Tom." I found it interesting that the bully of a detective seemed to bark at everyone by their last names, and yet this Fireman Tucker called the detective Tom. "Or I don't know. No pulse, only posterior injuries. But this lady, Tabitha Chase, says she was like this when she arrived." Tucker motioned to me and the detective turned and set eyes solidly on me for the first time. Or, at least, he set eyes on my brown leather boots. It took about three long seconds for his eyes to travel up the rest of me to my face.

I was an awful mess—soaked through my brown wool coat and even through my sweater. My normally orangey-red hair felt slick against my forehead and I most certainly didn't feel like being ogled. "Yes, she was like this when I found her," I said for the third time, almost feeling doubt in myself for all the skeptical looks being thrown my way. "It was raining like crazy. I'm just glad I saw her in time to stop and call 911."

"In time?" Tom the detective raised his dark eyebrows at me.

I swallowed, the seriousness of the situation hitting me anew. Because I hadn't seen the woman in time. "I meant in time to stop. So I didn't run over her." My voice dropped and I bowed my head, trying belatedly to show some respect.

"You got an identity yet?" Tom the detective barked toward the three firemen. He didn't wait for an answer, but moved closer to the woman, and said, "Ah. The Doerksen woman. Another one of those witches."

My head snapped up. "Witches?" I couldn't help but ask. My aunt had told fortunes for a living, so it wasn't as if I was completely unfamiliar with the word. It just seemed so strange, hearing it out of the all-business detective's mouth, as if he should know enough to see through people like this.

Tom snapped his look back to me. "Do you know this woman?"

I shook my head without looking at her. "I'm not even from here."

"So you've never met Maple May Doerksen?" Tom asked again. Why didn't anyone in this town believe me? It wasn't as though I was the one who'd been a fortune teller in this town for over twenty years, charging people money to make up stories for them!

"I've never met Maple May Doerksen," I said, deadpan.

Before Tom the detective could question me further, a light-colored sedan arrived. It parked in the small gap of road left unoccupied by the firetruck and the detective's sedan, and that's when I noticed the lineup of lights down the road in the darkness. Traffic, it seemed, had accumulated, but unlike in the city where people would be honking their horns by now, people had gotten out of their vehicles and stood in a group at a distance, whispering about the scene in front of them.

The man in the light sedan was the "Mick" they had been waiting for. Mick wore a white lab coat and studied the body on the road while Detective Tom stood nearby, updating him with everything he'd heard from me and Tucker.

It seemed as though everyone had forgotten about me. When I shivered again from the cold seeping through to my skin, I sidled up beside the bearded fireman who had returned to his truck. "Excuse me? Do you think it's alright if I go now?"

He took one glance over my shoulder at my car. "Don't think you'd be able to, even if it was okay."

I turned and saw what he meant. Not only was my car blocked by the detective's sedan, but now there were a half-dozen vehicles lined up behind that.

I nodded my thanks and headed back to my car. The engine was still running, burning a lot of gas, and my headlights were still on. I got into my driver's seat, turned off my headlights and cranked up my heat. The firemen had set up three portable lights by this time, so I didn't think the absence of my headlights would make any difference, but the moment they flicked off, Tom's gaze snapped to my car and he marched straight over.

I unrolled my window as he said, "Where do you think you're going?"

I clearly wasn't going anywhere, but his tone made me angry. "I'm warming up! I'm soaked right through all my clothes and you gave me no idea how long I might be here, so I had no choice but to take care of myself."

Tom the detective nodded. "Take care of yourself." Again, his words made me feel like I was responsible for this horrible accident. He didn't stay to accuse me of anything outright, though. Instead, he strode to the front of my car, squatted, and started studying it with a flashlight.

This guy was too much.

Cold or not, I buttoned up my coat and got out of my car. I stomped around to the front. "Look, I told you I didn't hit that lady with my car. I've told you and your firemen three times, and I have no idea why you keep—"

He stood and got right in my face. "Well, if you didn't run into Maple May, why is there blood on your hood? Would you like to tell me that?" He shone the flashlight at my light blue Honda Civic, and sure enough, there was a streak of dark red across the front edge of the hood. "I'll bet you a million dollars if we test it, it'll match up with Maple May's blood."

My mind scrambled for an answer as I burned with anger. Had I hit the woman and knocked my head and forgotten the whole thing? Was I completely delusional? But then my answer burst out of my mouth the second it came to me. "That was from me! My hand." Tom tried to interrupt, but I didn't let him. "I'd tried to take the woman's pulse...while I was on the line with 911. My hand got blood on it and I wiped it—"

"You wiped it on your car?" He raised an unbelieving eyebrow at me.

I waved toward the bushes. "No, Tom." If he was going to talk to me like I was stupid, I was determined to do the same thing back to him. "I wiped it on a napkin, but I guess I got some on my car. Yes, it will match that woman's blood, but no, I absolutely did not hit her with my car!"

Tom took his flashlight toward the bushes. When he located the offending napkin, he pulled out a small plastic Ziploc with the word "Evidence" emblazoned on the side. I resisted the urge to roll my eyes. After all, if these people still chose to believe I hit the woman with my car, I didn't have a lot of ways to prove otherwise.

After that, Tom took a swab of "evidence" from the front hood of my car. He turned to me when he was done. "I'll need your driver's license and registration, please, Ma'am." I bent into my car to retrieve them, but not before he spoke his next words to me. "And I'd also love an explanation for why you think it's appropriate to call me Tom."

Order Witchy Wednesday now at books2read.com/witchywednesday!

Join My Cozy Mystery Readers' Newsletter Today!

Would you like to be among the first to hear about new releases and sales, and receive special excerpts and behind-the-scene bonuses?
Sign up now to get your free copy of **Mystery of the Holiday Hustle – A Mallory Beck Cozy Holiday Mystery**.

You'll also get access to special epilogues to accompany this series—an

exclusive bonus for newsletter subscribers. Sign up below and receive your free mystery:
https://www.subscribepage.com/mysteryreaders
Turn the page for a recipe from Mallory's Recipe Box...

From Mallory's Recipe Box: New Orleans Po' Boy

THE PO' BOY SANDWICH can be made with a variety of meat, seafood, or vegetarian fillings, but crunchy golden shrimp are my favorite. Coupled with a fresh slaw and the remoulade, it makes the perfect combination for a satisfying meal. French sandwich rolls can be substituted for your favorite hero rolls.

Ingredients

1 pound medium shrimp, shelled, deveined and with tails removed

3/4 cup fine yellow cornmeal

3/4 cup flour

½ teaspoon cayenne pepper

½ teaspoon dried oregano

½ teaspoon dried thyme

½ teaspoon garlic powder

1 tablespoon kosher salt

½ teaspoon freshly ground black pepper

2 eggs, beaten

Vegetable or peanut oil for frying

1/2 head iceberg lettuce, shredded

2 to 3 tomatoes, sliced about 1/4 inch thick

4 French sandwich rolls, sliced lengthwise

Remoulade

1/4 cup Creole mustard

1 1/4 cups mayo

2 teaspoons prepared horseradish

1 teaspoon pickle juice or vinegar

1 teaspoon hot sauce of choice

1 large garlic clove, minced and smashed

1 tablespoon sweet paprika

1 to 2 teaspoons Cajun seasoning

Instructions:

1. Blend all ingredients to make the remoulade sauce. Mix well and let the mixture rest.

2. Prepare the shrimp coating: Mix the cornmeal, flour, and seasonings in a large bowl. Lightly whisk eggs in a separate bowl.

3. Dredge shrimp: Working with a few at a time, dredge the shrimp in the egg, then in the cornmeal-flour mixture.

4. Fry shrimp: Pour enough vegetable or peanut oil in a large frying pan to come up ¼ inch, and set the pan over medium-high heat until

a small amount of flour sizzles when you drop some in. Shake off any excess breading and fry the shrimp until golden on both sides, about 2 minutes total. Set the fried shrimp aside on paper towels to drain. Crispy shrimp is a staple of this recipe, so be sure not to crowd the pan.

5. Assemble sandwiches: Smear the remoulade on the top and bottom half of each roll. Place a layer of shredded lettuce on the bottom of the sandwich, then arrange the shrimp on top. Lay 2-4 slices of tomato on the shrimp and press the top of the bread down on the bottom, compressing the sandwich a little.

Serve at once with a side of hot sauce and enjoy!

Acknowledgements

Thank you to my amazing team of advance readers, brainstormers, and supporters. I am so very thankful for every single one.

Thank you to my developmental editor, Louise Bates, my copyeditor, Sara Burgess, my "Strange Facts Expert" Danielle Lucas, my cover designer, Steven Novak, and illustrator, Ethan Heyde.

Thank you for joining me, along with Mallory, Amber, Alex, and Hunch on this journey. We're thrilled to have you along on this ride!

THE MALLORY BECK COZY Culinary Capers:

Book 1 – Murder at Mile Marker 18

Book 2 – Murder at the Church Picnic

Book 3 – Murder at the Town Hall

Christmas Novella – Mystery of the Holiday Hustle

Book 4 – Murder in the Vineyard

Book 5 – Murder in the Montrose Mansion

Book 6 – Murder during the Antique Auction

Book 7 – Murder in the Secret Cold Case

Book 8 – Murder in New Orleans

Find all the Mallory Beck novels at bit.ly/MalloryBeck!

Collaborative Works:

Murder on the Boardwalk

Murder on Location

Saving Heart & Home

Nonfiction for Writers:

Writing with a Heavy Heart
Story Sparks
Fast Fiction

Denise Jaden is a co-author of the Rosa Reed Mystery Series by Lee Strauss, the author of several critically-acclaimed young adult novels, as well as the author of a few nonfiction books for writers, including the NaNoWriMo-popular guide Fast Fiction.

Her new Mallory Beck Cozy Culinary Mystery Series will continue to launch throughout this year. In her spare time, she acts in TV and movies and dances with a Polynesian dance troupe. She lives just outside Vancouver, British Columbia, with her husband, son, and one very spoiled cat.

Sign up on Denise's website to receive bonus content (there's a new clue in every bonus epilogue!) as well as updates on her new Cozy Mystery Series.

www.denisejaden.com

Made in United States
North Haven, CT
10 March 2023

33856637R00125